Joanna

SpringSong ❦ Books

Andrea

Anne

Carrie

Colleen

Cynthia

Gillian

Jenny

Joanna

Kara

Kathy

Lisa

Melissa

Michelle

Paige

Sherri

Joanna

Elaine Schulte

BETHANY HOUSE PUBLISHERS
MINNEAPOLIS, MINNESOTA 55438

Joanna
Elaine L. Schulte

Library of Congress Catalog Card Number applied for.

Lines from "Morning Has Broken" in *The Children's Bells* by Eleanor Farjeon, Oxford University Press, reprinted by permission.

Grateful acknowledgment is made to David Highham Associates Limited for permission to use copyrighted material.

ISBN 1–55661–624–4

SpringSong edition published 1995
Originally published under the title
Whither the Wind Bloweth by Avon Books.
Copyright © 1982
Elaine L. Schulte

Published by Bethany House Publishers
A Ministry of Bethany Fellowship, Inc.
11300 Hampshire Avenue South
Minneapolis, Minnesota 55438

Printed in the United States of America

To Joanna, Matt, and David.

Broken wings can soar again,
shattered voices can sing anew
with wondrous beauty
before unknown.

ELAINE L. SCHULTE is the well-known author of thirty novels for readers of all ages. Over one million copies of her popular books have been sold. She received a Distinguished Alumna Award from Purdue University as well as numerous other awards for her work as an author. After living in various places, including several years in Europe, she and her husband make their home in Austin, Texas, where she writes full time.

1

Something terrible is going to happen, Joanna Stevens thought as she waited alone at the school bus stop. Shifting her armload of books, she peeled off her brown cardigan, and the sun was immediately hot on her arms. A bad omen, such heat on Halloween morning, she decided.

It was the blasts of hot wind whipping through the eucalyptus trees that felt so fierce. The towering trees reeled like crazed dancers against the cloudless blue California sky, branches bending and silvery green leaves fluttering wildly.

Devil winds. Santa Anas. She'd read about them. They swept fires across southern California every fall, bringing out arsonists and other crazies. Some people claimed that the winds brought on suicides. Strange . . . back home in Kansas, people were expecting winter, and here in Santa Rosita, people expected fires and suicides!

The gusting wind muffled the sound of a car until it stopped right in front of her. She looked up, amazed to see Matt Thompson smiling widely at her from his bright red Corvette.

What's he doing here? she wondered, pulling back windblown wisps of her brown hair. Matt lived over by the ocean, on the other side of Santa Rosita. Why would he drive here?

He leaned across the seat as he opened the door for her. "Joanna, my lovely. I was in the neighborhood and knew you were dying to go to school." He grinned. "Want a ride?"

"Sure, thanks." She almost laughed at his come-on as she hopped in. Everyone knew that Matt was forever jumping from one beautiful girl to another. So what had prompted him to stop for *her*? He was tall, thin, a sun-bleached blond, and dreamily handsome—a popular senior, very big on campus. She was an unknown junior, new here from Kansas. Since the first day of school, she'd hoped he would notice her.

"If you're wondering why I'm in the neighborhood," he said with a straight face, "I had an important medical consultation. I'm a world-renowned expert on heart palpitations, you know."

"*Really*, Dr. Thompson," she said. She'd seen Matt in a starlight community play in August—he could act, he could sing, he could dance. What's more, he was a top student and captain of last year's winning basketball team. But an expert on heart palpitations?

He was staring straight at her, completely serious.

"Really!" she said again, and before she knew what had happened, he was trying to kiss her.

Astonished, she pushed away, catching her breath, not knowing what to say.

He sat back and inhaled deeply, rolling his green eyes and holding a hand over his heart. "Now that's what I call heart palpitations," he intoned dramatically.

She couldn't help laughing. No one could help liking Matt and his crazy humor. Quite a few girls at school were madly in love with him. Anyhow, he hadn't meant it to be a serious kiss. There was no sense in trying to fool herself. It was only part of his constantly changing act.

"Well," he said, grinning at her again, "onward to school. We'll teach the teachers what's what."

"Great idea," she agreed.

From the corner of her eye, she saw her neighbor David Porter hurrying down the road toward the school bus stop. "Maybe we should give David a ride. It's so hot."

"No way, my lovely. No way!" Matt expertly maneuvered his Corvette onto the street, leaving a trail of gray dust. "He's one of those religious nuts."

She gave David a quick wave, and he waved back through the dust. He looked surprised to see her with Matt Thompson. Wouldn't everyone!

"You know, my lovely, I'm going to put you in the movies. I have connections. I'll make you a star."

"I'll bet," she answered. Everyone knew his mother had been in movies, but surely he was just kidding. "Do you say that to all of the girls?"

He smiled, watching her more than his driving.

She wished he'd keep his eyes on the road instead of on her. All he could see anyway was a small brunette with big brown eyes. People said she was pretty, but she wasn't so certain.

"Wondering what I have in mind, eh?" he asked, grinning at her like a villain.

"You're crazy!"

"You've got it!" He grabbed her hand and kissed it loudly, again and again. "Would you like to go with me to Melanie Tillinghast's party tonight?"

She laughed. She could hardly believe this: Matt Thompson, kissing her hand like a mad comedian and, at last, her chance to be part of Melanie's group—the popular kids, just as she'd been in Kansas all through school. "Sure, I'd like to," she said, hoping she didn't sound too anxious.

His act continued all the way to school, and she knew she hadn't laughed so much since she moved to Santa Rosita in August. Nothing this year had been so much fun.

When they pulled up in the school parking lot, three of Matt's friends yelled, waving him over and looking surprised to see Joanna with him. Others in the parking lot turned toward them as if the word were spreading. Who could miss any girl with Matt in the bright red Corvette! She tried not to seem too pleased.

In the distance someone called out, "Leave it to old Matt to check out the newest chick. We've got to move faster."

"Yeah, but he never gets himself tied down," someone answered.

She glanced at Matt, wondering if he'd heard. He was smiling, but his green eyes didn't meet hers. It seemed like a warning: not to count on him too seriously.

"See you tonight at seven-thirty," he said, sliding out of the Corvette gracefully for such a tall guy.

"Okay." She let herself out and shut the car door carefully.

"I'll be ready," she called after him. But he was already heading for his friends, yelling about the weekend weather for a sailing trip to Catalina Island.

She smiled at the kids who glanced at her. Everyone would know that she had a date with Matt Thompson. Maybe she wasn't popular yet at Santa Rosita, but Matt was the first step, and Melanie's party was the second. The day felt as exciting as the blasts of hot wind.

Heading up the stairs toward the Spanish-style school, she glanced at the white stucco buildings with their red tile roofs. They'd been built years ago. At first they had seemed so foreign, but now they felt just right.

After two lonely months, she was becoming a real part of Santa Rosita High!

Just last night she'd told her mother about the three groups at school: the popular group, who seemed a lot wilder than the teens back in Kansas; the boozers and stoners, who were burning out their brains with alcohol or drugs; and the big crowd of people in between. *Strange*, she thought. In Kansas she had been a cheerleader, class vice-president, secretary of the student council, honor roll student . . . and popular. Here she was part of the big middle group—entirely out of it and not at all where she wanted to be.

She hurried through the crowd for her outdoor locker. She wouldn't be "out of it" much longer. Not after Melanie's party. Matt's invitation was a thousand times better than her best daydreams.

As she pulled her American lit. book from her locker, she remembered she hadn't asked Matt what to wear. After all, it was Halloween. Maybe they were supposed to wear costumes. She stood, biting her lip, then recalled that Melanie was usually around the French classroom first period. Slamming her locker, Joanna rushed to find her.

Melanie was just coming around the corner, surrounded by her friends. She looked tan and beautiful, as cool as a fashion model should. Her long black hair was coiled loosely around her head, and thick black lashes encircled her violet eyes.

Does she wear violet contact lenses? Joanna wondered. The color was distracting. As for Melanie's little violet dress, it would have been outlawed in Kansas schools.

Joanna stood on tiptoe to call over the crowd. "Melanie?"

Melanie glanced toward her, then away to her friends.

After edging her way through the crowd by the French classroom, Joanna arrived just as Melanie turned to go in. "Melanie . . ." She reached out to touch her shoulder.

Melanie turned indignantly.

"Matt invited me to your party tonight, and he didn't say if we should wear Halloween costumes or what—"

"Matt's bringing *you*?"

For a moment Joanna couldn't think what to say. "I hope that's all right," she finally stammered.

Melanie smiled haughtily. "Well, it's not a children's party, you know. You could wear that costume you have on now." She turned and stalked into the classroom with her smiling friends behind her.

Joanna felt the stares of nearby students. Her face flaming, she headed for American lit. Sudden tears stung her eyes and clung to her lashes, and she willed herself not to cry. *Maybe Melanie is right about this outfit,* she thought. It had been perfect last year in Kansas: brown and cream plaid skirt, cream blouse, and brown cardigan. But her old clothes didn't really fit in at Santa Rosita. Nothing she did seemed to fit in. If only her family had never moved to California!

She bit down on her lower lip, but it didn't stop her burst of tears.

2

*J*oanna hurried across the school patio to American lit. The only good thing about the wind, she decided, was it quickly dried tears.

She glanced around. Everyone was busy with his or her own life. No one noticed her at all. No one even cared. Worst of all, she still didn't know if she was supposed to wear some kind of costume to Melanie's party.

The hot wind buffeted bursts of red bougainvillea blooming across the school's old white walls. *If only the wind would stop,* she thought as dry blossoms and leaves rustled across the sidewalk. It made her feel edgy. Was it the wind that made Melanie act edgy, too?

Well, it wasn't worth crying about anyhow, she told herself firmly. She was not going to let Melanie spoil the day or her date with Matt. She headed for her classroom.

"Hey, Joanna!" someone called from the back row as she stepped into the room.

She glanced back. It was Chad Chandler, one of Matt's friends and co-captain of the football team. "Hi," she answered.

He grinned, then turned to some of his friends, no doubt spreading the news of her ride with Matt . . . and maybe about their date tonight. None of Matt's friends seemed to have noticed her before this morning. She sat down in her front-row seat. Maybe she could switch to a seat in the back. All the popular kids sat back there.

Heidi Matthias plopped an armload of books onto the desk next to Joanna's. "Missed you on the bus this morning."

"I had a ride," Joanna said, hoping that Heidi would ask who had picked her up.

Heidi lifted her long blond hair off her tan neck. "It's so hot today! I thought maybe these Santa Anas were too much for you, and you were still in bed."

"No. Not quite."

Joanna thought that was just where she would like to have been when Melanie snapped at her. "It's weird, though, to have hot weather at Halloween. I'm not used to it."

"Devil winds." Heidi slid into her seat. "Devil winds and Halloween. Sounds like bad spirits running amuck, doesn't it?"

Joanna shrugged, then couldn't resist telling her. "Matt Thompson's invited me to Melanie's party tonight."

Heidi's eyes widened. "Bad spirits all right."

"What do you mean?"

"Should think before I talk," Heidi replied, "but, seriously, watch out for Melanie. She's like a wild mustang that doesn't take to taming. She's—"

Joanna interrupted, "Should I wear a costume to Melanie's party?" She didn't want to hear Heidi's usual talk about horses, and she didn't want to hear any criticism about Matt's friends.

Heidi shrugged. "Better ask Matt. They'll laugh at you if you're the only one in costume . . . or they'll laugh if they're all wearing costumes and you're not. I don't know what's in with them nowadays. The only thing I know for sure is that their rules are always changing. You have to be fast on your feet to stay on that track."

Joanna wasn't too surprised. She glanced out the door thoughtfully. The students passing by struggled against the wind just as she had been struggling to fit in at this school. The wind whipped their hair, shirts, and skirts until everyone looked unreal. Today everything seemed so strange.

"I've never really thought of people being like horses."

Heidi raised her blond brows. "I guess I do a lot. You know, plow horses, quarter horses, thoroughbreds, and beautiful wild mustangs . . . like Melanie."

"Yes, I guess I can see her as being a little like that," Joanna decided.

"Wild mustangs are beautiful, but they don't fit in well among people. I guess I'd rather be a thoroughbred."

Joanna knew what she meant—a strong, kind person. She gave a laugh. "What am I, a plow horse?"

"No. Not at all." Heidi smiled thoughtfully as she dug her American lit. book out of her leather backpack. "I'm not sure yet about you. You haven't settled in," she said with a little laugh just as the class bell rang.

Opening her book, Joanna wished she could be more like Heidi in one way. Heidi knew her goal: to go to the best vet college in the country. Most of the other juniors at Santa Rosita High were thinking about college already, too. And Joanna hadn't even settled into high school.

She sighed quietly. Right now she'd have to forget about her future and about Matt and Melanie. Right now she'd better concentrate on this class. Mrs. Ekelman was already discussing Edgar Allan Poe's "The Cask of Amontillado." Poe had been a crazy genius. Like Matt.

At lunchtime Matt stopped by her locker. "Joanna, my lovely!" he exclaimed as if he were amazed to find her there. "Come along to see old Matt's noontime performance."

She subdued a giggle as he grabbed her hand and hurried her to the patio next to the auditorium. It was protected from the wind, and everyone was congregating there. Other students turned, surprised to see them together, but she pretended that it was normal, even to be expected.

"Madam," he said, bowing her onto a patio bench with a great flourish.

Melanie arrived in her daring violet dress. "Well, here I am," she said. "This had better be good."

Matt beamed. "It is! It is!" He escorted her to the bench beside Joanna with the same grand flourish.

Joanna and Melanie smiled uncertainly at each other, but Matt was already beginning his act—a macho imitation of Mr. Zale, the football coach, striding up and down the sidelines at a game.

A crowd gathered, laughing in appreciation. "Go, Matt!" someone yelled.

Matt seemed to become Mr. Zale, strutting around like him, imitating his voice to perfection as he bellowed out orders.

He is funny, Joanna thought. She glanced at Melanie. Melanie's mind seemed far away and hovering around something grim. Her hands were tightly clenched in the lap of her violet dress.

"Isn't he a riot?" Joanna asked.

Melanie came to and forced a small smile. "Yes. Matt's a riot." Her eyes softened slightly. "Matt's okay." She spoke the words as if she were his older sister, and for an instant Joanna hoped she and Melanie could be friendly.

Just then, two of Melanie's friends stopped at the edge of the crowd and waved her over. Applauding Matt, Melanie dipped a theatrical little bow back at him and started toward her friends.

Joanna had a feeling that Melanie and Matt played these theatrical games often. She watched Melanie hurrying away, cool and sophisticated. Everyone said that Melanie did a lot of fashion modeling for photographers in Los Angeles, and it was easy to see why. She was about as beautiful as anyone could be.

Joanna turned back to Matt's performance. More people were gathering, and they roared with laughter as Matt imitated Mr. Zale trying to dance to rock. "Go, Matt, go!" they yelled, and he loved it.

Later, while the fun of Matt's act lingered and everyone was drifting away, Joanna asked him, "Am I supposed to wear a costume to the Halloween party?"

He glanced at her sharply. "No way! And it's not a Halloween party. Melanie doesn't do anything that common." He must have realized that he'd hurt her feelings because he quickly joked, "You would be ze laughingstock."

"I'd be ze disaster," Joanna answered breezily. She could see from the concern in his green eyes that she had better not be an embarrassment to him tonight at the party. She would have to be careful.

That afternoon, as she waited in the school bus crowd, she wondered if Matt would stop by to give her a ride home. She pressed against the wind, holding down her brown plaid skirt—her costume, as Melanie had called it. Yet since they had watched Matt together during lunch hour, some of the sting had gone out of Melanie's words.

Oh, where was he? She finally got on the bus, dreading the dull ride home. Unfortunately, Heidi took a different bus home on Fridays so she could help at the animal care center.

"Hey, Joanna!"

She glanced up the bus rows. It was David Porter, her neighbor, sitting near the middle of the bus.

"Hey, I saved a seat for you!"

His voice came out so loud that she couldn't ignore him. He was a sophomore, kind of cute but gawky. He looked as if he'd grown so quickly that he couldn't figure out what to do with his arms and legs. He was nice, though—but as Matt had explained, David Porter was a religious nut.

He was standing up to give her the window seat. His dark-blond, wavy hair was windblown, and his glasses had slipped halfway down his nose. "I'm glad you're coming home on the bus," he said, seemingly unaware that the kids at the back of the bus were laughing at him.

Maybe he thought Matt had lost interest in her already. "Yes, well, Matt has to get going on arrangements for a party tonight."

David blinked hard, looking at her strangely.

"Thanks for the seat," she finally said.

They glanced out the window in silence. Suddenly she saw him—Matt in his bright red Corvette and Melanie with him! They were stopped, waiting for traffic to pass.

Joanna couldn't take her eyes from them. She saw Matt look with a terrible yearning at Melanie as he asked her something. Melanie turned to him with an indignant look, as if to say, "Don't be ridiculous!"

Joanna turned away quickly, then saw the concern in David's eyes. She tried to smile off the whole scene. "The party tonight is at Melanie's, you know. Matt will be helping her get things ready. They've been friends since before first grade."

David smiled kindly. "You don't have to worry about her. She doesn't go out with younger guys." He was quiet for a moment. "That's not gossip either. She says she won't go out with anyone under twenty-five."

"You're kidding!"

"Well, she's almost nineteen. She lost a half year of school when she lived in Europe. She graduates in January."

"Who told you she doesn't date anyone under twenty-five?"

"When high school guys ask her out, that's what she tells them. She said the same thing to a couple of college guys, including my cousin."

"Maybe it's just a kind way of letting them down." She watched Matt's car take off through the parking lot traffic and roar down to the road.

"I don't know," David said. "I heard she's mad about a famous golf pro in L.A."

"How on earth would she get to know a famous golf pro?"

David's face turned red. "He used to date her mother."

Her mother! Joanna watched the red Corvette disappear down the road. She had heard amazing stories about Melanie's mother, who'd been divorced four times. Someone had called her the playgirl of Santa Rosita Hills.

David was certainly embarrassed about the whole subject, she thought as the bus finally took off. She glanced at him sideways.

His eyes were closed, his long lashes dark against his fair skin. As he opened his eyes and saw her watching, a blush rose again on his face. "I hope you have a kind way of letting boys down, too . . . because . . . well, this is really last-minute. Anyhow, I wondered if you'd go to a senior high church party with me tomorrow night. It's at my house."

He sounded so confused, Joanna knew she didn't dare smile. Maybe it was the first time he'd ever asked a girl for a date! What could she say? She didn't want to hurt him, but she didn't want to go, either. Maybe Matt would ask her out—if he didn't go sailing.

David was still smiling at her. "You can just say no if you don't want to go."

"I do want to," she found herself saying, "but I'll probably be busy."

"Yeah," he said. "I figured you'd rather go out with Matt. It's okay."

It didn't seem okay at all—David looked crushed. "Actually, it depends on the weather," she explained. "Matt may be out sailing this weekend."

David brightened. "Oh, the weather will be great for sailing. But I'll call you tomorrow morning to check in."

"Okay." She sat back, and they looked uneasily at each other.

"Is it a costume party?" she asked. This time she would find out from the beginning.

"No. Just a party. Actually our church doesn't go for Halloween parties with witches and devils and all of that."

Did they think that there was something bad about witch and devil costumes? she wondered. Maybe he belonged to a weird church or even to a cult! "Why don't you wear those kinds of costumes?" she asked.

"It doesn't make sense for Christians to get involved with celebrating a night given to witches and demons."

"I guess I can understand that," Joanna decided aloud. She recalled her grandfather telling her about

God and Jesus when she was little; sometimes she wondered if the memory was only her imagination. Anyhow, she would rather talk about something else. Religion was for little kids and old people. "Tell me about the party," she said.

David grinned. "It's just a monthly party. We have parties or trips to Disneyland or go to movies or something every month. Last summer we went to Alaska on a mission."

A mission! Was he a missionary?

"What's it like in Alaska?" she asked, hoping to stop any missionary talk.

The rest of the bus ride home he told her about Alaska—about great humpbacked whales, sea lions, glaciers, and icebergs. It sounded as if they'd had fun, but then he didn't discuss the missionary part of it.

He was still telling her about their adventures in Alaska when they stepped off the bus into the hot gusting wind. They walked up the leaf-littered blacktop road to the hillside development of new Spanish-style houses. As they reached Joanna's driveway, he laughed at himself. "Afraid I really got wound up."

"It was interesting," she said to be polite. To be honest, though, she hadn't really been bored. "Goodbye, David."

"I'll call you," he replied.

She headed for the black wrought-iron gate in the white wall around her backyard. A strange feeling made her glance to the road above that wound up to David's house. He had stopped and was looking down at her. She thought for a moment that he was praying. Could it be that he was praying for her?

The next moment, they both waved and she hurried on.

She jumped over the eucalyptus bark and twigs

whirling at her feet. So far, it had been a good day despite the devil winds and her early-morning premonition. But what would her family think about Matt? And what would Matt think of them? She wanted everything to be perfect. She opened the gate leading to the backyard and the Mexican tile patio.

Shaded by the patio table's yellow umbrella, her father and a strange man sat in the colorful webbed chairs. "Hi, baby!" her father exclaimed. He stood up, grinning crookedly, then reeled and was laughing. "Come on," he sputtered, "meet my new friend." He staggered and sat down hard in the chair.

Joanna forced a polite smile at the stranger. He looked bedraggled, as if he had been picked up out of an alley, but so did her father. They were both drunk, terribly drunk. *How could he do this again?* she thought bitterly. He had been sober for more than a year. He had promised over and over that he wouldn't drink if they moved to California.

Her mind raced as she walked toward them. Her little sister, Cathy, would be home on the grade school bus in half an hour. She shouldn't see Dad like this. Their mother wouldn't be home from work until five-thirty. Oh, why did he have to ruin everything!

An empty liquor bottle lay in a planter box and a half-empty bottle stood on the table near their glasses. The wind whipped Joanna's hair across her face, reminding her of her premonition. She'd known something terrible would happen today.

"Joanna, baby," her father was saying, "this is my friend—" He laughed, his handsome face red and blotchy. He turned to the stranger. "Wass your name?"

Something in her didn't want to believe that the man before her was her father. He usually looked so handsome, so neatly dressed for his job as a computer salesman; but now his graying hair was wild, his white shirt rumpled, and his blue eyes were red and watery.

"Pretty little thing," the man said. "I'm partial to brunettes with big brown eyes."

Joanna backed away and was glad to hear the phone ringing inside. "I'd better answer the phone. Excuse me." She whirled and ran for the back door, then slammed it behind her. Grabbing the kitchen phone, she gasped, "Hello."

"Joanna! I hoped you'd be home," her mother said nervously. "Do you know where Dad is? His office called me here, trying to locate him."

She could see the two men through the window. If only she could wish all this away. If only she didn't have to tell her mother! If only . . .

"Joanna?" her mother asked, more alarmed.

Joanna took a deep breath. "He's drunk."

She was empty, detached, as if this time it were happening to someone else's family. "He and some—some man—are out on the patio . . ." She felt like crying. "Oh, Mom, I finally have a date tonight. With Matt Thompson. He's picking me up at seven-thirty!"

There was a long silence, and she felt embarrassed. She was putting her date first; she was being selfish, more concerned about herself than about her whole family. But if only they knew what a dream Matt was.

Her mother's voice flattened. "Lock yourself into your room. I'll be home in fifteen minutes."

The memory of her father in a drunken rage, slapping her face hard, made her rush to her room and lock the door. She didn't want to remember and tried to push the bad memories away.

She went to her open window, feeling hot air blasting down the dry hills to the house. She closed the window quietly and drew the leafy green and white draperies, then she stood still, absorbing the silence.

It was such a beautiful room, she thought, trying to concentrate on that. White walls and dark beams on the ceiling. The leafy green and white bedspreads on the twin beds matched the draperies, even the wallpaper in her adjoining bathroom.

The decorator had sold them the hanging baskets of ferns and the potted plants in their Mexican terra cotta containers. The room looked like a garden with a fluffy white carpet. Why couldn't life here be as lovely as her room?

She closed her eyes. They'd have to hide her father's drinking problem again—hide it from his boss and the neighbors. And what if Mom had to quit her new job? She couldn't just stay home taking care of Dad. They'd spent so much money buying this furnished model home, not to mention her father's new Buick. Her mother had to work now, although she seemed to like her job as an executive secretary at an electronics company.

Well, she had better pick up her room, Joanna decided. At least it would be done for tomorrow. Saturday was cleaning day. She picked up clothes, organized skirts and pants and shirts in her closet and straightened the bookshelf wall.

How could time pass so slowly? If only she could see the driveway from her window. At last, she thought she heard a car door slam.

Moments later her mother was whispering at the door, "Joanna?"

She opened the door.

Her mother's face, white and pinched, looked older, and her brown eyes were wide with worry. Tendrils of brown hair had escaped her usually neat, upswept hairdo. "I want you to go out the front door and take my car. Here's money and a grocery list. Pick up Cathy at the school bus stop and take her to buy those white moccasins she's been wanting."

Joanna stared blankly at the keys and the list. Last week her mother had told Cathy they couldn't afford the moccasins, so this was an excuse to keep Cathy out of the house.

"Hurry! And don't come home until five o'clock," her mother said. "That'll give you time to get ready for your date."

She felt her mother propel her toward the front door.

"And don't tell Cathy. Or anyone else."

"Okay, Mom." Joanna suddenly kissed her. "I'm sorry . . . I'm so sorry."

"It has nothing to do with you, honey. Now go!"

Joanna rushed for the front door and out into the hot wind. Her mother's green minivan was already turned around.

As Joanna drove the minivan down to the school bus stop, she wondered if her mother had been arranging life around her father's drinking problem all of these years. She remembered her parents fighting in Kansas, her mother's black eyes, her father throwing her across the room. . . . She'd hated him so!

She made her mind stop rerunning the memories she'd hidden away for one good year. She wouldn't ever let Cathy know. Ugly memories were hard to forget.

Pulling up near the bus stop, she saw Cathy's yellow school bus in the distance. She turned off the ignition and glanced back up the hill toward her house.

Leaves and branches littered the road curving up the hillside. Some of the Spanish-style houses in the forty-house subdivision were almost hidden by the wildly blowing eucalyptus trees. Her house, halfway up the hill, white and lovely with its red tile roof, looked as serene as her room. The white stucco wall curved around the back patio. For the first time she felt grateful for the wall. Whatever was going on in her backyard was hidden.

The school bus braked to a stop, and its doors flapped open. Cathy was first off the bus. Her brown eyes opened wide with delight when she saw Joanna. Cathy's best friend, Dede, was right behind her. From a distance they looked almost like twins—except that Cathy was shorter and not as skinny as Dede. Both of them had brown hair cut in bangs and braided into fat pigtails, and both wore white blouses and jeans. The only difference in their outfits was their shoes: Dede wore her white moccasins. Now Cathy would have hers, too.

Joanna hoped that her sister would never know why. Leaning over to open the car door, she called, "Cathy! We're going shopping for your moccasins."

Cathy's brown eyes sparkled with surprise. "Really?"

"Yep." Joanna couldn't help smiling, Cathy looked so pleased.

Cathy turned to Dede. "I'm really going to get them!" She climbed into the minivan, yelling to Dede, "I'll call you when I get home!"

"Buckle up," Joanna told her.

"I'm buckling, don't worry," Cathy said. "How come you're picking me up—"

"Did you have a good day?" Joanna interrupted as they pulled onto the main road behind the bright yellow school bus. She'd divert Cathy's attention. There was no need for her to ever know what was happening at home.

3

$\mathcal{J}$ust after five o'clock Joanna and Cathy stepped into the house. Serene stereo music swirled through the air as they made their way with the groceries through the Mexican tile entry and family room. There was no sign of their father or the other man.

In the kitchen their mother turned to smile at them as she put an apple cobbler into the oven. She'd let down her long brown hair and brushed it. It made her look younger, but her brown eyes were dull. She seemed too subdued. Had she taken tranquilizers?

Cathy rushed into her mother's arms. "Thank you for my moccasins!" When she stepped back she pointed a foot to show them off, then gave her mother another hug. "I didn't think I'd get any."

Mom kissed the top of Cathy's head. "Don't be too loud, dear. Your father was so tired that he went straight to bed."

How had she managed that? Joanna wondered. Had she slipped him some of her tranquilizers?

Joanna set her bags of groceries on the white counter. If only Dad would sleep through the night! If only she could get away without introducing him to Matt tonight. Best not even think about it.

"I've got a date with Matt Thompson," she announced as she began to put the groceries away. "You know, the guy we saw acting at the starlight theater?"

"You're kidding," Mom said.

Joanna's spirits lifted as she told them about Matt picking her up at the bus stop and his invitation to Melanie Tillinghast's party.

"You mean you're going to the Tillinghast house?" her mother asked, impressed. "Well, I almost wish that I could go to your party. You know, their house was featured in a national architectural digest. They have all sorts of benefit parties. Famous people come there to raise money for charities."

Were they that rich? Joanna wondered uneasily. They lived "behind the gates," which meant there were security men guarding the gated private roads into Santa Rosita Hills. Her parents had checked out a few houses there with a realtor, but they were far too expensive.

Matt's family had lived in Santa Rosita Hills all his life until last year, Heidi had told her. After his parents' divorce they'd sold the house, and he and his father had moved to the beach. His mother and two sisters had moved to Palm Springs, and his mother had married again—this time to a much younger man.

"You'll have to give me a report on the house," her mother was saying, "although I expect my curiosity will kill me with envy." She laughed. "Maybe you'd better not tell me about it!"

"Oh, Mom, we have the most beautiful house in the world," Cathy put in. "Anyhow, *I* love it. And I love you!" She hugged her mother hard, as if she sensed something were wrong that had nothing at all to do with the elegance of the Tillinghast house.

After supper Joanna rushed to her room, glad that her father wasn't awake. She'd wear the new red dress she'd bought with her birthday money the Sunday her family had driven across the border for their first look at Mexico.

She carefully pulled the dress out from the back of her closet. It was perfect for tonight, just what girls here would wear—California casual.

An hour later she smiled at herself in the full-length mirror in her bedroom. With her brown hair freshly washed and blown dry, her tan, and the new leather sandals, she finally looked just like a California girl.

Cathy knocked at the door, then peeked in. "He's here, Joanna! Matt Thompson's here! He thought he told you seven o'clock."

"Shhh!" Joanna whispered in a panic. "We'd better not wake up Dad!"

Cathy glanced at her curiously. "Why not?"

"Go tell Matt I'm coming," she said, although it wasn't necessary. She grabbed her red Mexican string handbag and was on Cathy's heels in the hallway.

She thought she heard her father rattle the doorknob of her parents' room, then mutter groggily. Had her mother locked him in? she wondered as she hurried down the hall. *Oh, please, please don't come out and spoil everything!*

Matt and her mother were in the family room in front of the TV. The evening news blared out, but they seemed oblivious to it. Mom was beaming as if Matt had already charmed her.

"Hi," Joanna said.

Matt turned and stopped midsentence. "Wow, you look beautiful," he remarked, then thoughtfully added, "You look like your mother."

"Thank you." She glanced at her mother. How pleased she looked. He certainly knew how to get the better of mothers.

"You look beautiful, too," Joanna teased.

He laughed. He was wearing a natural cotton T-shirt and linen shorts.

She looked down at her red dress. "Maybe I'm dressed all wrong."

"Perhaps you'd better change, Joanna," her mother suggested, then turned to Matt. "What should Joanna wear?"

"That's perfect," he answered. "The girls wear things like that."

Anxious to rush out before her father stumbled in, Joanna hoped Matt was being honest. No time to change now.

She edged him to the front door as he talked politely with her mother and Cathy. He knew how to charm even little girls, Joanna thought. Cathy's big brown eyes sparkled with delight as she looked up at him.

She thought she heard her father down the hallway. "We'd better go, Matt."

He almost looked as if he didn't want to leave. Was he acting again? Although with his mother and two little sisters living in Palm Springs, which was hours away, maybe he missed having a family.

Matt tugged Cathy's fat brown pigtails, and she giggled. From the wistful look in his eyes, Joanna felt certain she'd guessed right. He missed being around a real family.

"See you," he said to Cathy, then bid Mom goodbye. He *did* have nice manners.

As they walked out to his red Corvette, he smiled ruefully. "Forgot my wallet. We'll have to swing by my house. We have plenty of time anyhow."

"Sure." She wondered if he'd help her into the car, but he went around to his side, his thoughts seemingly far away. Something was very wrong with him, she guessed.

They were on the main road before he glanced at her. "Hello there, my lovely! It's Friday night, and we're going to celebrate!"

Joanna laughed, relieved. She'd escaped without her father ruining everything for her with Matt. She'd escaped! And she felt wonderfully carefree. She wasn't even going to think about her father tonight.

"You'll have a chance to meet Rena," Matt said.

"Who's Rena?"

"Our house-sitter when Dad's out of town. Anyway, that's what he calls her. I'm supposed to be too old for baby-sitters. You know, she cooks and waits for repairmen and oversees the cleaning lady."

Sounds like a substitute mother, Joanna thought, then wondered if that had ever occurred to Matt.

On the way to his house Matt, crazy again, acted his way through what had happened to him and Melanie since kindergarten. They'd attended school camps together, riding and tennis camps. They'd even shared the same piano teachers and recitals. They sounded almost like a brother and sister, Joanna thought, yet she couldn't help feeling jealous.

As they pulled up to Matt's beach house in the darkness, Joanna was amazed. She'd expected a beach cottage, a battered bachelor pad for just Matt and his father. Instead, spotlights illuminated an ultramodern white structure that looked as if it had landed from outer space. There were porthole windows and roofs slanting from all angles. A white wrought-iron fence surrounded the yard, making the effect even more stark against the night sky. Tall palm trees, their green fronds flapping with the gusts of wind, made the house seem even less homelike.

She sat staring at the house so long that Matt came around to let her out of the car.

"Guess it doesn't look much like a Kansas house," he remarked.

"Oh, they have modern houses there, too," she protested, hoping that she didn't seem too stupid. "I've just never been in one."

The hot wind swept back her hair, and it occurred to her that this house seemed more suited to a desert than a beach on the Pacific Ocean. "It's very beautiful," she said, although unique was a better word for it.

They walked in through the back door, stepping into a white-and-black kitchen with gleaming stainless steel cabinets, refrigerator, and counters. The kitchen felt eerie . . . cold . . . not like anything she'd ever seen except in magazines, and her eyes were drawn to a basket of oranges, lemons, and limes for their warm colors.

"This way," Matt said. He led the way through the house to the enormous front entry with its carved double doors. A white metal staircase curved upstairs through the two-story entry. "Just make yourself at home," he said, then started up the stairs.

"Thanks."

She glanced around the entry hall. Above the double doors was a great round window like a porthole. A ship's porthole seemed perfect here with the muffled roar of the ocean in the house, but the house did not feel in the least like a home.

Joanna sat down uneasily on a bench and glanced at the enormous oil painting behind her. It rose halfway into the second floor of the entry. Mostly white, the painting had swirls of lavender and purple spiraling into mustard green dots. *Expensive,* she thought. Abstract and beautiful in a haunting way.

Straight ahead, the white living room was lit by

spotlights and white lamps with mushroom-shaped shades. Steel and glass tables held lamps and glass ashtrays among the white leather and steel furniture. Stainless steel mobiles dangled in museumlike splendor between other huge abstract paintings. It seemed unreal, as if the Thompsons lived in a futuristic world without flowers or trees or rivers or gardens.

It was taking Matt forever to find his wallet. Joanna stood up and wandered to the living room, then came to an abrupt stop. The far wall held a great window overlooking the ocean, and floodlights lit the huge dark waves rolling in across the distant sand.

It was a few moments before she noticed the older blond woman in the white dress reading near the window. "Oh, I'm sorry," Joanna said, backing away.

The woman turned and rose to her feet with a slow smile. "You must be Matt's new friend."

"Yes."

"I'm Rena," the woman replied softly, extending a hand.

Rena's eyes seemed to engulf Joanna. How beautiful she was. She was older than Joanna's mother, but her eyes seemed young and joyous.

"I'm Joanna."

Rena was still holding her hand. "I know. I know a great deal about you."

How could she? Joanna wondered. Matt didn't know much about her.

His footsteps pounded down the stairs, then he was behind them, stuffing his wallet in his pocket. "I guess you two have met. We'd better get going."

"It was nice meeting you," Joanna told Rena.

Rena smiled. "Maybe Matt will let me cook dinner for you two some night."

"Good idea," Matt said. "I'll take you up on that. See you later, Rena."

Outside, he said, "She's something else, isn't she?"

"Yes," Joanna agreed. "There's sort of an aura about her, as if she's reflecting a golden sunset."

"Come on!" he laughed. "A golden sunset?"

"Well, something beautiful and wonderful. . . ."

"Maybe," Matt said. "Maybe."

It was a while before she noticed that he had changed his clothes. Instead of the T-shirt and linen shorts, he had on a blue denim shirt and tan chinos. "You changed!"

He grinned. "You noticed."

Had he changed so that she wouldn't look out of place? Maybe he was more thoughtful than she'd imagined.

They didn't discuss Rena during the dark drive to Santa Rosita Hills, yet the white room, the ocean's muffled roar, and Rena's serene smile stayed with Joanna. She was still thinking about her as they pulled up at the lighted gatehouse leading into Santa Rosita Hills.

"Evening, Matt," the elderly uniformed guard said. "Glad to see you." The light from the gatehouse slanted across his smiling face.

"Hi, Hank. We're going to Melanie Tillinghast's party."

"Saw your name on the list," the guard said, pushing the button to open the road gate. He glanced at Joanna and nodded as he waved them on. "Have a good time."

Joanna caught her breath, excited to be in the gated community of Santa Rosita Hills. She looked about as their headlights pierced the darkness. Orange groves on either side of the road here and there, white wooden fences along riding trails, driveways with impressive entry posts and gates. In the distance, towering eucalyptus trees swayed with the wind against the night sky. *Heidi lives here somewhere,* she thought, watching for the Matthias name on the few entry gates that were lighted. She wondered if Heidi would be at the party. After all, she'd known Melanie for a long time.

No, she decided. Heidi probably wouldn't come even if she were invited. Heidi didn't seem to care about being popular at all. Strange to be more interested in horses than in popularity.

Matt drove into a driveway that curved gently uphill between rows of small subdued lights. Twenty or so cars were already parked nearby. "Guess this is as close as we'll get," he said, and parked the Corvette.

"Close enough!" Joanna answered—brightly, she hoped.

As they made their way up the driveway, she could hardly believe the magnificent two-story Tudor house that sprawled across the top of the hill. In the glow of night lighting, the lawns and hedges appeared to be perfectly manicured, as though a crew of gardeners groomed the estate daily.

"The party's back by the pool," Matt said, although anyone could hear the beat of rock music thumping out from behind the house. "Sounds like a great party. Melanie's mom and grandparents are out of town as usual."

No adults? Joanna wondered. At home in Kansas, parents usually hung around at teen parties.

As they stepped through the gate, Joanna saw the lighted Olympic-sized pool. A group of boys swung a bikini-clad girl by her arms and legs, back and forth, back and forth, until they let fly. She landed in the shimmering blue water with a splash and everyone laughing.

Someone was bouncing on the diving board—Chad Chandler from her American lit. class. His jet black hair was wet and curling, his face split in a wide grin as if he were delighted to show off his athletic physique. Joanna couldn't help noticing his muscular shoulders and arms as he dived in. "I didn't know we'd be swimming," she said to Matt. "I didn't bring a suit."

Matt darted a surprised glance at her. "There're always extra suits for guests in the cabana dressing rooms."

"Oh. Sure." She should have somehow guessed that swimsuits would be provided for guests.

She looked at the white building on the near side of the pool. Cabana. That had to be the cabana. There were doors all along it and, in front, a table presided over by a bartender in a white jacket. She hoped she wasn't gaping, but it looked like a movie scene.

"Hello, hello, hello!" Matt shouted over the blaring music. He danced in crazily. "You didn't wait for us to start partying."

"Man, we got started drinking out on the parking lot at noon," a boy yelled.

"You started drinking in fifth grade," another answered, starting a chorus of laughter.

Joanna smiled, feeling everyone's eyes turn to her. What were they thinking? Maybe Matt was making a big entrance, but the spotlight was on her.

She glanced at Matt, noting his look of approval. The red dress was just the right thing to wear after all, no matter what anyone else wore. This was her entry into the popular group.

She quickly took in the setting. The huge Tudor house was to the side of the patio. The cabana lined the near end; on the other side stood a high wall covered with billowing lavender bougainvillea. The far end of the patio was open, giving a view of shimmering city lights.

Melanie, with a swirl of her long purple dress, appeared from one of the patio tables to greet them. "Hello, hello, hello, yourself," she said to Matt with a proprietary smile. She glanced at Joanna as if it were an afterthought. "Hi."

"Hi," Joanna answered. It occurred to her that Melanie always averted her violet eyes quickly from her.

Matt stood back, grinning. "For a girl whose name sounds like a melody, you're sure looking like a dirge."

"Same to you," Melanie answered with a tense smile. "Same to you."

He bent to whisper something into her ear, and she shrugged. "I don't want to think about it tonight," she replied. "Anyway, he'll be here. He's flying in for the party."

Who was flying in? Joanna wondered. Melanie's golf pro?

Melanie nodded toward the bar. "Go get yourselves a drink."

As they headed for the bar, Joanna asked him, "Who's going to be here?"

"Her boyfriend . . . friend, I mean." Matt did not look happy about it.

They stopped in front of the bar, and Joanna tried not to look surprised. There was bottle after bottle of gin, vodka, and bourbon as well as mixes, just as her parents had served at parties. But here some of the kids were only fifteen . . . only sophomores at school.

Matt was watching her. How naive he must think she was.

"I don't touch the hard stuff," he was saying. "How about having some Italian white wine with me?"

She felt a sudden panic, never having drunk anything alcoholic. It was bad enough with her father. . . . Yet they'd laugh if she asked for a Coke.

Matt and the bartender waited for her answer. Well, she could pour the drink out when no one was watching. "Yes, some Italian white wine sounds lovely."

She accepted the glass of wine from the Mexican bartender, who eyed her quizzically. Perhaps she hadn't sounded as sophisticated as she'd hoped.

Matt had already sipped from his glass. "Hey, Juan, just give us the rest of that bottle," he said. "I'll save you from drinking it all yourself."

Juan laughed heartily. "*Gracias!*" He picked up his own drink and toasted Matt with it.

"Come on!" Matt grabbed the bottle and led the way toward the patio table, moving with the beat of the music. "A good party, huh?"

"It looks great," she answered. It really was like a scene from a glamorous TV show or movie, and she could hardly believe she was here.

They sat down at a long wooden table with nine or ten others. "Hey, Matt," the guys said, welcoming him. They looked Joanna over almost as carefully as the girls did.

She could sense them slowly accepting her. After all, she was with Matt Thompson, and he was entertaining them with something hilarious that had happened last year at a party. Joanna glanced around quickly. What could she do with her wine? No place to dump it. She thought Matt had forgotten about her for a long time until he returned with the wine bottle. "Need a refill?"

She glanced at her full wine glass, then smiled. "I forgot all about it."

He was waiting, wine bottle in hand, and several of the others were watching now, too.

She lifted her glass to him and sipped the white wine as if drinking were an everyday occurrence. It tasted surprisingly good. Not at all vinegary as she thought it might be. Looking over her glass at him as coolly as if she were in a commercial, she said with just the right tone, "So light and delightful."

Everyone laughed, and Matt refilled her glass.

Someone was passing a joint, but she waved it on smoothly, then was glad to see Matt pass it on without a drag. Lots of teens everywhere were smoking pot, not just in California.

After a while she wondered if it was the wine or just being with Matt that made the party such fun. Girls and guys who had never said a word to her included her now. She'd made it! She'd made it with the popular group here at last. Someone turned up the stereo, and she was wildly dancing with Matt and nearly every other guy there, stopping only to gulp more wine.

It seemed only minutes later that everyone was laughing as Matt and Chad grabbed her arms and legs and swung her threateningly over the pool.

"Let me get into a suit!" she yelled, then she was flying through the air, splashing into the bright blue water, red dress and all. She struggled to the surface, her wet dress heavy in the water. At least the water was warm.

Darting everyone an indignant look, she swam slowly to the edge, pulling herself out. "I'm going to get into a suit." She turned to ask Melanie's permission, but Melanie was not around. Strange . . . she hadn't seen her since the beginning of the party.

"Just take off your dress," Chad yelled, laughing. "I'll help!"

"No!" She struggled with them. "Stop it! Stop it!" she shouted just in time.

Laughing, they grabbed her arms and legs again and swung her into the pool.

She came up gulping the warm water and saw them

waiting for her. She swam rapidly to the other end of the pool, her dress dragging in the water.

She climbed out of the pool and dashed for the dressing rooms in the cabana. Finding an open door, she rushed in and locked the door behind her. She stood there, hearing the boys' laughing voices. It sounded as if they'd given up. What could she do now?

She opened cabinets and found a drawer full of two-piece bathing suits. A yellow bikini looked as if it might fit. She slipped it on and looked in the mirror, amazed. She had never worn such a daring suit, but she looked good in it. Perhaps now Matt would pay more attention to her.

Someone banged on the door. "Come on!" he yelled. "Let's see our new chick!"

She unlocked the door and, taking a deep breath, stepped out into a chorus of whistles and suggestive remarks. Where was Matt?

"If you're looking for Matt," Chad Chandler said, "he's probably out with Melanie. Old friends, you know. Old friends help each other." He called out to the others, "Aren't Matt and Melanie old friends?"

"Yeah!" someone answered. "Yeah!"

Joanna tried to smile as though she didn't care. "Come on," she said. "I'd like another drink."

Chad put an arm around her. "You look a lot better than Melanie ever did in those suits."

"Never mind!" she snapped, wishing he wouldn't eye her like that. She turned away and hurried to the bar.

The evening became a golden haze of drinking, dancing in the starlight, and occasional dips in the pool. She vaguely wondered where Matt was, then decided he was rotten for leaving her. She noticed couples disappearing into the darkness beyond the pool, some with a bottle, others with who-knew-what?

What if Matt were out there in the darkness with Melanie? No! She couldn't bear to think about it!

"Come on, Joanna," Chad was saying as they danced. "Let's go for a little walk." He was slowly easing her away from the lights, across the grass. "Come on," he said urgently. He grabbed for her roughly, and she slid just out of his grasp and dashed away.

She ran wildly, but he was closing in on her. Suddenly he cursed, tripping over a flower bed and falling with a thud.

Frantic, she ran for an open sliding glass door in the house. A bedroom with a light glowing from the adjoining bathroom. She crept into the room and slid the door shut behind her. Locking it, she caught a deep breath. Safe.

Glancing around, she found a dark corner and went to sit down on the carpeting, exhausted. Chad could just cool off before she went out there again.

After a while she crawled toward a small window above a built-in desk. There was just enough light coming in to see the books on the desk . . . Melanie's school books . . . Melanie's room.

Joanna stood up to look out the window. From this distance the party looked different than when she'd been in the middle of it. A few couples danced wildly to the music blaring out into the night; others were in the pool; some sat at tables. Someone was heading across the lawn for the pool. Chad. He rushed to the edge and dived in.

Relieved, she stepped forward, tipping something over. It made a metallic clunk. She waited, paralyzed, wondering if anyone in the house had heard.

No one came. No sounds in the house anywhere.

Reaching down, she found Melanie's wastebasket

on its side, papers spilling out across the carpeting. She brushed the papers together and put everything back into the wastebasket. She ran her hand across the carpeting again to see if she'd missed anything, and her fingers touched a scrap of crumpled paper.

A voice in the hallway startled her. Melanie?

Joanna grabbed the scrap of paper, rushed to the sliding glass door, and let herself out into the darkness. She started toward the swimming pool and saw Chad still swimming.

And there was Matt! He yelled, "Everyone drink up! Last drink!"

Where had he been? He was obviously looking for her, then saw her coming out of the shadows. "Well, my lovely," he said, "one more drink." He grabbed her hand and led her to the bar.

He didn't seem drunk, she thought, although she was still floating. She noticed his pants legs. Dry stickers clung to them here and there. Had he been hiking? Maybe hiking over the hill? He was talking to the bartender, something about Melanie wanting him to close up the bar.

Where had he been with Melanie? she wondered. Suddenly she was aware of the crumbled scrap of paper in her hand. Turning her back to them, she opened it and, in the dim light, read the wrinkled words, "I don't want to go on. I can't do it again."

The other words were torn off.

Joanna froze. What could it mean? A composition for Melanie's English class. . . ? or something else logical? She crumpled it in her fist. How could she explain taking a note from Melanie's wastebasket? Everyone would think she'd been snooping around in Melanie's room.

Matt handed her a glass of wine, and she gulped it.

"Hasn't it been a great party?" she asked. She tried to sound cheerful, but the words fell flat like stones.

"Drink up," he called out to everyone.

She drained her glass quickly, hoping it'd make her forget Matt's being gone most of the evening . . . and Chad's chasing her . . . and whatever it was that Melanie had written. Especially if it was what it sounded like—a suicide note!

4

*J*oanna awakened to the faint smell of smoke the next morning. She sat up groggily, glancing around her bedroom. Everything seemed fine. In fact, everything looked almost perfect. She remembered straightening up the room yesterday afternoon.

As she sat there, her head throbbed dully. Could she have a hangover? Of course not.

She got up and headed for the bathroom medicine cabinet and took two aspirin. Her dress, hanging on the shower bar, was almost dry now, and she vaguely recalled the guys trying to pull it off. No! She didn't want to remember too much.

The smell of smoke was stronger. Hurrying to her bedroom window, she pulled the leafy green and white draperies aside. The sky was tinged a garish pink. Fire! Somewhere beyond the dry hillsides not too far away, a fire burned.

"Joanna?" Cathy whispered, knocking softly on the door.

"Just a minute." Joanna pulled her pink robe on over her white cotton nightie. "Come on in."

Cathy bounced into the room in her flowery summer pajamas. "Did I wake you up? I want to hear all about your date with Matt. He's so handsome!"

"When we find out where the fire is," Joanna said. She didn't want to think about Matt—nor about

44

Melanie's note. Seeing the sudden fear on Cathy's face, Joanna wished she hadn't mentioned the fire, either.

"Mom and Dad are watching TV to find out about the fire," Cathy answered. "It's on lots of stations."

"Let's go see," Joanna said, leading the way to her door.

In the family room, their parents were watching television coverage of the fire all right. "It's way up in the foothills," Dad explained, "nothing to worry about." Except for the bloodshot eyes and puffiness under them, he looked fine, as though nothing unusual had happened yesterday.

It occurred to Joanna that he always appeared to be in control of everything. Maybe the doctors in Kansas were wrong about his being an alcoholic. Alcoholics were weakling types, street bums—not her father.

"They have airplanes dropping chemicals on the fire," her mother remarked. "It's supposed to be out soon." She shook her head. "I can't believe that people would actually set an enormous fire like this on purpose."

"Crazy fools," her father said. "They'd have to be crazy."

Her mother nodded. Had she already forgotten about yesterday afternoon? Joanna wondered. Wasn't it crazy for Dad to get drunk when he was supposed to be working? And wasn't it crazy for him to bring home a weird stranger?

She glanced at her father. He seemed a different person today. It was almost as if he had a split personality—one good and one awful.

At breakfast Cathy wanted to know all about Matt Thompson. "Did he try to kiss you? Did he?"

"Oh, Cathy!" Joanna protested, blushing. Little sisters could be so exasperating. The worst part of it was that Matt hadn't tried to kiss her at all.

"Well, did he?" Cathy asked.

"Never mind, Cathy," Mom put in. "You won't want us asking questions like that when you're older."

Joanna glanced at her mother gratefully, then noticed her father's angry stare.

"I should hope that my daughter isn't kissing boys," he said. "I expect you girls to be dignified."

Dignified?!

Of all the nerve, Joanna thought. What right did he have to ask her for dignity after *he'd* gotten drunk yesterday!

"Just to quiet everyone's curiosity," she said, "I was not kissed, and I did not kiss anyone!" She stood up quickly from the table.

"Come on, honey," Mom said. "We don't mean anything by it. It's just that we love you. Let's drop the subject and have a nice breakfast."

Joanna sat down. She tried to eat the sausages and scrambled eggs, but her stomach churned. Why did they have to ask if Matt kissed her when he hadn't even tried?

She remembered last night's scene at the door. He'd walked her to the front door and waited while she unlocked it. When she turned with an expectant smile, he said, "See ya, my lovely." And he'd rushed back to his car.

For a moment she'd stood staring in amazement. He didn't want to get involved, that's what it was. Maybe it had something to do with Melanie.

"Did you have a good time?" her mother asked now.

"Yes. Yes, thanks," Joanna answered. But as she recalled their date, she wasn't sure. She'd scarcely seen Matt all evening, and when she had, he'd seemed vaguely disinterested in her. He'd probably never even ask for another date.

"Do you feel well, Joanna?" her mother asked. "You look pale."

"I'm fine," she answered, forcing down a bite of sausage. It tasted awful. Her stomach lurched, and nausea rose to her throat. "I guess I don't feel so well after all. Excuse me." She got up and ran for her room.

Did she have the flu? she wondered as she lay down. Or maybe it was the smell of smoke from the fire. Whatever it was, she felt awful.

"Joanna! Telephone!"

She opened her eyes, realizing she'd slept. Ten o'clock!

"Coming, Mom."

Maybe it was Matt, she thought. Maybe he hadn't gone sailing to Catalina after all. She hurried out to the hall phone. "Hello."

"Hi, Joanna," the masculine voice said.

Her heart leaped.

"This is David. How are you doing?"

It was a moment before she recovered from disappointment.

If he noticed, it didn't seem to bother him. "Hope you can make it tonight," he said.

Oh no! She'd meant to make up an excuse to get out of his church party tonight.

"Can I pick you up at seven-fifteen?" he asked. "Everyone will be coming around seven-thirty. I should be back here then."

She felt trapped. But why not go? It was better than sitting home. Anyhow, Matt would probably never ask her out again. "Sure, David," she answered, trying to sound pleased. "Seven-fifteen is fine."

"If you get bored this afternoon, maybe you could

help me decorate for the party."

"Decorate?" Hadn't he said that they didn't get involved with Halloween?

"We're using the Alaska trip theme," he explained. "We've got posters and that kind of stuff."

"Oh well, sure. If I get my work done. I have to help clean house on Saturdays." She was embarrassed as soon as she'd mentioned it. Almost everyone had at least a cleaning woman once a week. David's family had a live-in Mexican maid. His mother had just become an attorney and said she'd never clean house again.

David didn't seem to notice. "Okay. If you get your jobs done, come on over."

"Thanks."

If only it were Matt, she thought as she hung up.

It was four o'clock before she finished her chores. Why not help David decorate for his party? It was something to do. Cathy had just finished with her jobs, too, and was ready to go to Dede's house.

"You want a ride?" Joanna asked. "Maybe Mom will let me use her car for a while."

"Wow! Okay!" Cathy said. "But I always walk."

"I just thought it might be fun to drive today. I'm going to help David decorate for his party tonight. I could walk up the hill to his house, too, just as easily."

"Driving would be wonderful," Cathy said, her eyes glowing with admiration.

It was difficult to be as admirable as her little sister saw her, Joanna thought. In fact, it was almost impossible.

As they stepped into the kitchen, her mother gasped from where she stood on the white counter. She grabbed an open cabinet door for balance. "You scared me! I'm just cleaning a little."

Why would she be cleaning up there? Joanna wondered. The top cabinet shelves were full of punch cups, extra coffeepots, Christmas cookie tins—things they rarely used. She peered around her mother and saw the long necks of liquor bottles. So that was it—she'd taken the liquor from the built-in bar and hidden it up there.

Joanna pretended not to notice. "Can I take your car to David's for an hour? I could drive Cathy to Dede's, too."

"Sure." Her mother pretended to be calm as she closed the cabinet doors and climbed down from the counter. "Just be home by five. I'll get dinner started early. Have fun!"

Joanna wasn't sure it would be fun, but it'd definitely be better than staying at home.

The hot Santa Ana wind was still blowing as she rang David's doorbell. She stood at the Porters' carved Spanish door, glancing around. Just below, she saw their new swimming pool. David said they kept it heated all year with solar panels. Far below, eucalyptus trees swayed near her own house.

A sliding glass door opened on the lower level, near the swimming pool. David stepped out, smiling. "Down here, Joanna. We're having the party in the rec room.

"I'm glad you came," David said as she made her way down. "Just when I need help, too."

He showed her in through the sliding glass door, and she looked around at the brightly decorated room. Green and blue beanbag chairs, a well-used couch, and a big blue throw rug in the middle of the room. Bouquets of enormous, brightly colored paper flowers like the ones she'd seen in Mexico gave the room a festive air. Posters of Alaska hung on the wall.

"Looks like a mix of Alaska and Mexico, doesn't it?" David asked. "Anyhow, it's cheerful. The Mexican flowers are from one of my parents' parties."

"It looks great," she said. It did. "How can I help? Everything looks ready."

"Over here." He led her to the back wall. "I found this Alaska mural on clearance at a wallpaper shop. It's a little beat-up, but . . ."

Joanna helped him unroll the enormous mural. It was an Alaskan scene of green tree-covered islands in a bright blue waterway; the background was snowcapped mountains and a great white glacier. "Whoa! It's beautiful."

"It's the Inland Passage where we were. I figured it'd cover a lot of the back wall, and when everyone walked in, it'd be just like walking back into Alaska."

"It must have cost a fortune," she said.

"No. The shop owner gave it to me. He's a Christian."

"Gave it to you? He just *gave* it to you?" she asked. Even though it was frayed around the edges, a mural that big was expensive. No one ever gave *her* things like that!

"I've got these long strips of wood to frame it onto the wall," David said, then explained how he wanted to put up the mural.

After they fastened it to the wall, they stood back to admire their work.

It did make the room seem as though they had stepped into Alaska, Joanna decided. "Won't your mother be upset about putting nail holes in the wall?"

David smiled. "I know it sounds crazy, but I sort of own the downstairs of the house."

"You own it?"

"Well, my grandfather paid for half of the house, and he willed it to me. He always used to joke that he owned the downstairs. See, he lived here before he died, and he had his room downstairs. Now the maid uses his bedroom. It's back there." He nodded to the other side door.

"You mean, he died since you've lived here?" Joanna asked, not quite believing it. David's house couldn't be more than two years old. All the houses in the development were fairly new.

"Yeah. Last year," David answered.

"I'm sorry, David. I shouldn't have asked."

"Oh no, it's okay. He's in heaven. I'm one hundred percent sure. He was a minister, you know."

A minister?!

No wonder David was religious.

He grinned. "Actually a wonderful thing happened when he died. He was right in that room down the hall, and we had a full-time nurse. He'd been in a coma for a month. Well, I used to come in and just sit with him after school. Have you ever seen anyone in a coma?"

"No. Never." As for being wonderful, the whole thing sounded gruesome to her.

"They don't talk or open their eyes or anything. Well, you probably knew that. Except on Gramps' last day. He was just lying there quietly as usual. He had beautiful white, wavy hair; he was very distinguished looking, to give you an idea."

David quieted, remembering. "I was sitting beside his bed, when all of a sudden he smiled! He really smiled and opened his eyes."

David looked full of wonder, as if it were happening before him again. "Then he waved. He actually waved! I asked him who he was waving at, and he said, 'Don't you see them? Don't you see them?' He looked so thrilled! Then his head fell back on his pillow, and he was dead. But he was still smiling."

"You're kidding," she said, wondering whom

David's grandfather might have waved to. Maybe old friends and family on the other side—if there was another side. She'd never thought much about it.

"It's the truth," David protested. "Have you ever been around dying people?"

Joanna shook her head. "No. I've never even been to a funeral. My grandparents were killed in a car accident when I was little, and my parents didn't want me to see them dead."

"That's too bad," David said. "I mean, about the accident. I'm glad I got to know Gramps. He's been the most important person in my life."

Joanna wondered if David might someday be a minister, too.

"I'll never forget him smiling like that and waving," he said. "Never. That was when I—" He glanced at her, suddenly self-conscious. "Now how did I ever start talking about that? Come on, let's go upstairs and get the chips and dips ready."

That was when David did what? she wondered. She followed him up the stairs. They didn't discuss the matter further as they helped the Porters' maid with the food.

―――――

That evening Joanna was waiting in jean shorts and a peach-colored T-shirt when David came to pick her up. At least there'd been no problem about what to wear.

"I didn't drive. I hope you don't mind walking," he said. "We can enjoy the sunset better."

He was different, she thought, glancing up at the sky. It was a beautiful sunset, all right—awesome in a frightening way. The sun shining through clouds of smoke turned the sky a brilliant pink and lavender, and here and there red streaks slashed through like comet tails.

"I've never seen a sunset like that," she said.

"It's because of the fires," he explained. "Even bad can come to good."

She glanced at him, wondering. Most guys didn't get so involved with sunsets. And what did he mean? *Even bad can come to good?*

They turned as they heard a car behind them. It pulled up beside them, and she vaguely recognized two of the five kids in it from school. "Want a ride to your own party, David?" the driver asked.

"Sure." David started to climb in. He looked embarrassed when he realized that Joanna would have to sit on his lap. "Maybe you'd rather sit in front."

The girl in the front seat opened her door, and Joanna squeezed in. David was introducing all of them, and she tried to be very polite; but she wished she were with Matt, not here.

As they pulled up at David's house, two more cars joined them. Everyone piled out of the cars and headed for the rec room. Most of them, she noticed, wore Alaska T-shirts.

Weren't David's parents going to be here either? Didn't California parents ever stay home for their teens' parties?

"Wow, look at that poster of Alaska!" one of the boys exclaimed.

"Where'd you get it?"

David explained about the Christian shop owner giving it to them, and they didn't seem at all surprised.

Joanna guessed that Christians stuck together, at least sometimes.

Another car pulled up outside. "Hey, there's Gary," someone said, pleased.

Joanna looked over at the man with the dark, curly hair as he made his way in. He was probably about thirty. He greeted everyone, then did a double take at the big Alaska mural on the far wall. "Where did you get that? It's fantastic!"

David explained about the wallpaper shop owner's donating it.

"Fantastic!" Gary exclaimed again. After a moment, he began to visit with the kids as if they all were old friends, slowly making his way across the room until he was in front of her.

"I'm Gary," he said to introduce himself, "the assistant minister at our church."

Joanna suddenly felt very formal. "How do you do. I'm Joanna Stevens." She wasn't certain if she should offer to shake hands since she'd never met a minister. More than anything, she felt like escaping.

"Glad to meet you, Joanna."

He did look glad to meet her, she thought. And he almost looked like one of the kids, wearing a bright yellow Alaska T-shirt.

"Too bad you didn't go with us last summer," he added. "We had a great time . . . for some of us, the greatest trip we ever took. But you'll get to see the video." He talked for a moment longer, then excused himself to get the tape.

Three girls had brought scrapbooks of snapshots and souvenirs, and Joanna found herself looking at them. It did look as if they'd had fun. Last year, besides Alaska, they'd gone on trips to Disneyland and Magic Mountain in Los Angeles.

When she finished with the scrapbooks, she glanced around. There was something very different about these people—besides being religious—but she couldn't decide what it was. Maybe an air of excitement, but that didn't make sense.

A little later Gary banged a spoon against the big punch bowl. "Let's thank God for our blessings," he suggested. The room quieted, and he bowed his head.

Joanna saw David bow his head beside her, so she did, too.

"Heavenly Father," Gary began, "we thank you for bringing us together again tonight. We are especially grateful for the wondrous trip to Alaska, where, squeezed into that little boat, we surely became Christian brothers and sisters in closer ways. We thank you for this food here at David's house, and we thank you for every blessing you've given us. Help us always to reflect your love. We pray in Jesus' name. Amen."

"Amen!" several chorused.

Joanna especially noticed David's firm "Amen." Suddenly, she wanted to get away. Maybe they'd have a weird ceremony or something.

The party went on as if Gary's prayer hadn't even interrupted it. She was relieved when someone turned on the VCR and the lights were doused.

The video began with their crazy excitement at the airport and on the plane, then showed shots of their landing in Juneau. "Everything's so green," someone exclaimed. "I thought there'd be lots of snow."

The video showed them climbing a glacier, then singing at a nearby church. The trip went on, and they were singing to Alaskan Indians in a dilapidated church, to loggers at a lumber camp, to old people in a retirement home, to patients in a hospital.

Joanna felt less and less a part of them as they sang along with themselves in the movie. "What a friend we have in Jesus," they sang. "All our sins and griefs to bear . . ."

What sins could these kids have? They seemed too

good to get into trouble, and why couldn't they bear their own griefs?

There were shots of great humpbacked whales breaching high out of the ocean, thousands of sea lions, glaciers, waterfalls, icebergs.

When the video ended, David remarked to her, "I hope we didn't bore you."

"Oh no. It looked beautiful," she answered, even though the religious stuff turned her off.

"We're not sure yet, but maybe next summer we're going on a raft trip down the Colorado River."

"Who's not sure yet?" Gary asked from behind them. "Let's have a final vote on it tonight, and I'll get going on the arrangements." He turned to Joanna. "You're welcome to join us, of course."

"Oh, I couldn't do that," she said.

"Why not?" David asked.

Because she wasn't one of them, she thought. And she didn't want to be one of them, no matter where they might go!

"Anyhow, keep it in mind," David suggested. He turned to the others. "Hey, guys, let's eat!"

Joanna grabbed more chips, then sat back quietly as they discussed the raft trip and voted, eyeing them one by one. None of them were popular at Santa Rosita High as far as she knew, and she felt fairly certain that she'd know by now.

Someone began to sing softly. "Hallelujah . . . hallelujah." Others joined in until it sounded eerie. Soon they were all singing "Hallelujah" over and over. Some raised their hands as if to God while they sang, and Joanna felt more and more uneasy.

Gary began to speak into the soft chorus. "I like to think about heaven, not as an escape, but as the place that is truly our home. When we think about heaven, it brings us closer to Jesus here on earth."

Above the singing, a girl uttered, "We're pilgrims on a journey to heaven."

"We're on earth temporarily. Life is a spiritual journey to heaven."

If only I could get out of here without making a scene! Joanna thought.

"Heavenly Father, we adore you," a girl murmured into the "hallelujahs," then someone began to sing about power in the precious blood of the lamb.

They're crazy, Joanna thought, rising to her feet to escape. She could dream up an excuse for getting out later!

The phone rang on a nearby table and David grabbed it. He listened hard, his face paling. "Gary!" He all but shoved the phone into the assistant minister's hand.

David turned to Joanna, stunned. "You'd better sit down. It's bad news. It's—there's been an accident."

"What is it?"

"It's Melanie," he said. "I'm afraid that Melanie has . . . I'm afraid that Melanie has committed . . . suicide."

5

$\mathcal{G}$ary hung up the phone, his face as ashen as Joanna felt. A stillness hung over the room as if everyone sensed that something was wrong. "It's very bad news, gang," he said. "Very bad news. I can't even think of a gentle way to break it." He stopped, then went on. "That was the Tillinghasts' attorney. Melanie Tillinghast is dead."

Eyes closed with shock.

Gary shook his head. "A maid found her in bed at noon today. Melanie took . . . an overdose of sleeping pills." He grabbed a deep breath. "Her family has asked me to officiate at the service Monday afternoon. They've asked me to invite all her friends and classmates."

Joanna felt cold. She'd heard something about people who committed suicide—that they went straight to hell. Another thought struck. What she'd seen last night—even held in her hand—was Melanie's suicide note. If only she'd told Matt!

Everyone was getting up to make a prayer circle. David held out his hand to her, and a girl reached out to her from the other side. It seemed there was nothing to do but join in the circle and hold their warm, moist hands.

"Heavenly Father," Gary said, "you in your great wisdom know everything. It's not for us to judge

58

Melanie. But, Father, we ask your forgiveness if we could have tried more to help her, if we could have tried harder to tell her about Jesus. We thank you that your love can conquer all things—and that death is not final for those who love you."

After a short silence, a girl added, "Father, forgive me for not trying harder to be Melanie's friend."

Beside Joanna, his hand warm in hers, David prayed, "Help us to know from now on when anyone is that desperate. Help us to be more sensitive to others."

The prayer continued, but Joanna could only think how foolish it was now that Melanie was dead. They all should have done something long ago. She should have done something about Melanie's suicide note! She tried hard to focus on the prayer, but it didn't make sense. Hot tears slipped from her eyes.

When the prayer ended, she turned away, fumbling in her pocket for a tissue. No tissue. Sobbing, she ran for the bathroom.

Splashing cold water on her face, she finally got control of herself. When she stepped back into the rec room, no one seemed to notice her. People were too busy putting on their sweaters and jackets; some carried leftover food upstairs.

David came over to her. "We're going to church together tomorrow morning in remembrance of Melanie. Would you like to go along?"

"I don't know," Joanna began. Maybe it would be a good thing to do since it was in memory of Melanie, but something in her mind said, *Absolutely not! Don't go!*

She glanced up at David.

"It won't hurt you to go," he said, smiling.

"I guess not," she decided. "Okay, I'll go. But if you don't mind, I'd like to walk home alone now."

"Are you sure?"

He looked hurt, but she nodded.

"I guess I understand," he said, walking her out to the moonlit street. "At least it's bright out."

"Thank you for—" She couldn't very well thank him for a good time, but she saw that he understood. "It was fun till the phone call," she said. Maybe even that wasn't quite true, she thought, but she wanted to forget about the party and Melanie and everything else.

"I'll pick you up at nine-thirty tomorrow morning." She nodded and started down the road.

A few minutes later a car of teens from the party drove down the road toward her, and she ducked behind some bushes. No way did she want to ride with anyone now.

When she started off again in the moonlight, she wondered if Melanie could see her walking down the road. Was being dead like sleeping? Or, worst of all, was she burning in a lake of fire? A sudden vision of Melanie screaming from a pit of fire, red demons dancing around her, made Joanna run down the road for her house. She'd read about a fiery lake and demons somewhere.

She tried to wipe her mind clean of thoughts of Melanie and just concentrate on the stars glimmering in the sky—the Big Dipper, the Little Dipper, the North Star. If only she were still in Kansas looking up at the night sky. She had been so much happier there.

As she stepped into her house, she was surprised to find a light on in the family room and her mother still up, reading a book.

"You're home early," Mom remarked as Joanna made her way into the family room.

Joanna didn't think that she should tell about Melanie. It would only worry her. Having decided that, she suddenly blurted, "Melanie Tillinghast committed suicide! We heard at David's party."

"No!"

Joanna nodded. "Everyone was so upset that it broke up. . . ."

But Mom wasn't taking in the words. Instead, she looked terrified. What was she thinking—that Joanna or Cathy might kill themselves, too?

"It broke up the party," Joanna repeated. "They all prayed."

Her mother glanced at her sharply. Finally she managed, "That was nice."

Joanna decided to say it right now. "I told them I'd go to church with them tomorrow morning—in honor of Melanie."

Mom hesitated. "I guess it can't hurt to go tomorrow. I just don't want you making a habit of it. I've had enough religious grief in my life."

Joanna nodded. Mom's teenage sister, Annie, had joined a religious group years ago and refused to take her medicine for heart trouble. Annie had claimed to be healed—and she'd died.

"Why would Melanie do such a thing?" her mother asked now. "It sounded as if she had everything— money, modeling in L.A., a sports car, trips all over the world."

"Something was bothering her," Joanna said sadly. "Oh, Mom, why didn't I help her somehow?"

"How could you know?"

Joanna told her about Melanie's party, about her disappearing and her family not being there. She almost told about Melanie's note, but she couldn't. She just couldn't get it out.

"Where were Melanie's mother and grandparents?"

"Her mother was in Las Vegas, and her grandparents were at their home at Lake Arrowhead," she answered. But she wanted to cry out, *I was there! I should have helped!*

"You mustn't blame yourself, Joanna," Mom told her. "How could you have known?"

Joanna shrugged with dejection. "I'm going to bed."

At one o'clock she still hadn't slept. She tossed from side to side, thinking about Melanie and glancing at the digital alarm clock. Two o'clock, three o'clock. . . . She should have told someone about Melanie's note.

At three-thirty she decided she absolutely had to sleep. She'd promised David to go to church in honor of Melanie. After getting out of bed, she tiptoed to the kitchen and climbed quietly onto the kitchen counter. Opening the high cabinet where her mother had hidden the liquor, she found dozens of bottles of bourbon, gin, rum, vodka, and after-dinner liqueurs. She recalled her father's laughing about cream sherry. "A lady's drink," he'd said. "There's nothing to it."

She found a water glass and filled it half full of cream sherry. That much would surely make her sleep, she thought, then tasted it. Sweet . . . sweet like a dessert.

She closed the kitchen cabinet quietly, then tiptoed back to bed, trying not to feel guilty. After all, it wasn't hard liquor like her father drank. And the important thing was that she sleep.

The next morning she awakened groggy, vaguely aware that something horrible had happened. Melanie's suicide!

She dragged herself from bed, remembering she'd agreed to attend church this morning. She headed dully for the shower. *At least that will wake me up,* she thought, then took two aspirin for the headache lurking around her eyes. She saw the bottle of antacid tablets in the medicine cabinet. Maybe they'd take away her queasiness. She'd have to wear something dull . . . something solemn for church.

By nine-thirty she was ready in her tan dress and caramel-colored heels. As she stepped into the family room, she was glad that her father wasn't up yet. She definitely didn't want to explain about Melanie to him, too.

In the kitchen, her mother asked, "Don't you want breakfast? Your stomach will rumble in church."

"I don't care," Joanna said. "Well, maybe I'll have a slice of toast."

How pale and unhappy her mother looked. She wore the old blue robe she'd had on last night. "Are you sick, Mom?"

"I stayed up reading too late last night." She turned away to something over the range.

Her mother never stayed up late reading, Joanna thought. She was forever talking about keeping sensible hours. Was there something wrong with Dad again?

Cathy appeared in the kitchen behind them, rubbing her eyes sleepily. "Where are you going?" she asked, noticing Joanna's dress and heels.

"Church." Joanna bit into the hot buttery toast.

Cathy's eyes opened wide. "Why are you going to church?"

Joanna glanced at her mother, who shrugged lightly. "She's going to find out sooner or later. One of Joanna's classmates died," she explained. "Melanie Tillinghast."

"You mean, she's dead?" Cathy asked. "Really dead?"

"Yes," Joanna answered. "Melanie's dead."

"Why?" Cathy asked. "What happened to her?"

Joanna closed her eyes. "Would you mind if I ate my toast outside?" She rushed out, not wanting to explain it.

Closing the front door behind her, she inhaled deeply. Hot as it was, it felt good to be outside. She glanced at the swaying eucalyptus trees, and it occurred to her that it had been Friday morning, only two days ago, that the Santa Ana winds had begun. Matt had stopped by to drive her to school. It seemed impossible that life could change so much in two days.

Thank goodness, Matt would be home this afternoon, she thought. Unless something awful happened to him, too.

Concentrating on her piece of toast, she took a careful bite and forced herself to chew slowly. She must not think terrible thoughts.

She glanced up the hill. David's beat-up yellow car was coming down the road. He'd painted the car himself, and it looked like it.

Stopping, he leaned over to open the car door for her. "Hi. I'm glad you're going to church with us this morning."

Joanna climbed in and slammed the door. "Thanks." She was still unsure she wanted to go, but the car lurched forward. From everything she'd heard about church people, they were hypocrites. "Do your parents go to church?"

"Not always," he answered, a little embarrassed. "They were at a late dinner party last night, and they're sleeping in this morning."

She glanced at him sharply, expecting him to defend his parents, but he didn't. Well, if it weren't for Melanie, she wouldn't be going either, Joanna thought and stared straight out the windshield.

"We're picking up Shirley and Stan," he remarked. "I hope you don't mind." He stuck a tape into the tape deck.

How could she mind? Joanna thought, trying to ignore the taped praise music. What chance did she have to mind? She remembered Shirley and Stan from the party. Shirley had started singing "Hallelujah" as if she were already off to heaven. Joanna forced her attention to the eucalyptus trees reeling against the cloudless blue sky. Now, there was something real—Santa Ana winds and fires.

Shirley and Stan stood waiting in front of their house, smiling a little as David pulled up. How could they smile at all? Didn't they care about Melanie? Callous . . . that's what they were. They climbed into the back of the car, talking as if nothing were wrong.

Joanna decided she'd be solemn in honor of Melanie. If they didn't like her being quiet, that was too bad. Yet all the way to church no one seemed to notice—in fact, everyone seemed subdued.

In the church parking lot a car full of teens waited for them. Everyone got out when another car with people from David's party pulled up.

Joanna nodded distantly. Somehow she'd get through this morning, she thought. She headed with the others for the large white church, deciding it resembled an old Spanish mission.

As they approached, church bells pealed into the warm wind, and she followed the throng of people to the entrance and hoped none of Matt's friends would see her here—with David.

A young minister in a long black robe turned to her. "Good morning, Joanna. Welcome."

She was taken aback for an instant, then realized it was Gary, the assistant minister who'd worn the Alaska T-shirt at last night's party. "Good morning," she answered solemnly. He sure looked different in a long black robe.

At the edge of the crowd, a gray-haired minister in

a voluminous black robe smiled a welcome. Joanna felt like running, but David's hand was at her elbow. He gently guided her to an elderly couple who greeted everyone at the door, then into the church and the swirl of organ music.

As she looked into the white sanctuary with its huge, dark wooden beams, she panicked. Except for weddings, she'd never been in a church. What if she was supposed to kneel or cross herself or something? What if she didn't know what to do?

She glanced at David as they waited for an usher to come down the aisle to seat them. David smiled at her reassuringly, then she followed the usher up the middle aisle, wondering if everyone were looking at her. Stopping near the front, the usher handed her a program and she took it warily. The cover had a picture of Jesus on it; surely it was supposed to be Jesus. She sat down between David and Stan on the cushioned pew.

Settling back, she glanced at the program again. The picture on the cover was like no picture she'd ever seen of Jesus. He looked tough, like a thick-necked carpenter, not like the graceful statues at cemeteries. His picture seemed alive in her hand. His eyes looked into hers.

She quickly opened the program. Perhaps if she studied it now, she wouldn't do anything foolish, she thought. She glanced at a quote: "Come unto me, all ye that are weary and heavy laden, and I will give you rest."

Well, she was not weary, nor was she heavy laden, she decided, although it might be a nice thought for older people. And there were a lot of older people around her. They probably thought more about death than younger people would. Except for Melanie.

Hymnbook pages rustled as the organ began a new song. Oddly enough, she'd heard the song before.

David found the page and held the hymnbook out to share with her. Suddenly everyone rose to their feet and she was standing between David and Stan.

The music flowed through the church like a brilliant sunrise. "Morning has broken like the first morning . . . blackbird has spoken like the first bird . . ."

Yellow-robed choir members moved forward by twos down the main aisle; as they stepped slowly past the pews, their voices soared over the singing of the congregation.

Beside her, David was singing out about rain's new fall and the first dewfall.

The gray-haired minister now stood in the pulpit, and Joanna saw the enormous dark wooden cross on the white wall behind him. *Maybe these people think Jesus died for them,* she thought. *But why should He have died for me? I haven't done anything that wrong. And I never asked anyone to die for me!*

The minister read, "May Christ dwell in your hearts by faith."

Joanna mouthed the words on the program so she wouldn't look out of place. "That being rooted and grounded in love, we may have the power to comprehend with all saints, what is the breadth and length, and height, and depth, of the love of Christ."

It didn't make sense, she decided, then listened to the minister go on about being filled with the fullness of God. She gave it up. The prayer that followed seemed endless. Then they all were singing out, "Joyful, joyful, we adore thee, God of glory, Lord of love . . ."

Next came a Bible reading—something about Abraham, about Noah's building his ark by faith, about Enoch's being raised right up into heaven without dying.

These old stories were crazy. Even if they were

true—and that was unbelievable—it was centuries and centuries ago. What could it have to do with people now?

She glanced at David. How could he believe this? Had he and everyone else here been hypnotized?

There were announcements about a women's luncheon, Bible study classes, a potluck dinner. Then came more music, and ushers walked down the aisles with collection plates. Well, she was not going to give money for any of this, she decided. Besides, she was David's guest.

She watched uneasily as the collection plates were passed, coming closer to her, pew by pew. When a wooden plate started at their pew, it came to her with unexpected suddenness. Staring straight ahead, she took it and passed it on with a barely suppressed shudder. Up front, a blond choir member stood under the great brown cross singing about her friend Jesus. Her friend! About how this friend knew her deepest needs and had walked this way before her. That He would lead every step.

Then they all stood and sang as the money was brought forward in the collection plates. "Praise God from whom all blessings flow . . ."

It was understandable why Dad thought churches wanted nothing but your money . . . and why her mother thought it was better not to get too involved! She glanced at David singing out loudly about Father, Son, and Holy Ghost. She could imagine him wearing a minister's robe. She turned away. She would never get involved with anyone who was into religion again.

She thought about Matt, trying to imagine him on the sailboat, maybe leaving Catalina Island now, sailing home through the bright sunshine. How beautiful it would be out there. Would he ever invite her out sailing?

She'd taken sailing lessons one summer on a lake, but it was a long time ago. She'd probably remember what to do again. If only he'd ask her.

She looked up. The minister stood at the pulpit, talking about a great cloud of witnesses who had carried faith forward—he seemed to be gazing right at her. She glanced away quickly.

Finally they were singing the last hymn. It went on about Jesus Christ and then a verse about the Prince of Darkness. The devil? Did these people believe there really was a devil, too?

She glanced around during the minister's benediction. His right hand reached powerfully out above the people as he blessed them. Well, she did not want his blessing; she wanted out. She'd come only because of Melanie, yet not one word had been said about her!

"Did you enjoy the service?" Stan asked as they stood up to leave.

"It was all right," she lied. He seemed pleased.

David, Shirley, and Stan made small talk as they filed out of the church. When they quieted, Joanna turned to David. "Why didn't he even mention Melanie?"

He seemed perplexed. "No one in her family is a member of the church."

"But she's lived here forever. I thought that churches were supposed to be for the whole community."

"They are," he agreed, "but it's just like a—like a museum with a beautiful painting in it. If you don't go to the museum and reach out to the beauty of the painting, it doesn't do a thing for you."

She didn't want to hear about museums and paintings. Melanie must have had some connection with the church. "Didn't her family ask Gary to speak at her funeral?"

David nodded. "I guess they didn't know who else to ask. Melanie went to a church summer camp with us once in the mountains, but none of them ever came to church."

Isn't God for everyone? she wanted to ask.

It was the last straw when they walked out the door. The minister stood there, and it was impossible to avoid shaking hands with him. "I hope we'll see you here again," he said, his eyes meeting hers.

"Thank you," she answered, but her mind said, *No way! Never again!*

6

*M*att called at two o'clock that afternoon, his voice trembling. "Joanna, you've got to come over."

"Sure, Matt." He'd heard about Melanie, and he wanted her help! "I'll be there as soon as I can."

"Hurry. I'll be waiting."

She rushed to her room for her leather handbag and quickly brushed her hair, then hurried outside.

Her mother sat on the patio in the shade of the table's yellow umbrella. She glanced up over the Sunday newspaper and noticed Joanna's handbag. "Where are you going?"

"Matt called. He's awfully upset about Melanie. Can I use the minivan to drive there?"

Her mother frowned. "I don't think you should go. He'll think you're throwing yourself at him."

I don't care what it looks like, Joanna thought. "He called and asked me. It wasn't my idea."

"Well, you can't use my car. Dad took it to the office." Mom turned her attention back to the newspaper. "You'll have to use Dad's car."

Strange he'd be working on Sunday, Joanna thought, but there was no time for questions. "Thanks, Mom. Don't keep dinner for me . . . and don't worry."

Joanna remembered that Cathy was at Dede's house this afternoon. "At least it'll be a quiet afternoon for you, Mom," she said, kissing her mother's forehead. "See you."

She hurried into the house for the car keys and headed for the garage. She didn't like driving her father's new green Buick for fear of putting a scratch on it. She'd just have to be careful.

Driving along the coast highway near downtown Santa Rosita, she thought she saw Mom's minivan parked on a block of sleazy bars. Glancing in her rearview mirror, she saw a man who looked a lot like her father staggering across the sidewalk. No! Her father wouldn't drink at bars like that. Besides, he was working at his office. She tried to concentrate on how she could help Matt. Maybe, just maybe, he would get over loving Melanie someday.

As she pulled up in Matt's driveway, she remembered her first reaction to the house. Today the modernistic house had the same chilling effect. A moment later, Matt hurried out to her car as if he'd been watching for her. His hair was sun-bleached blonder than ever; his face, arms, and legs all the way to his jeans shorts were bright red with sunburn. He looked miserable . . . and not just because of his burn.

Climbing out of the car, she patted his hand awkwardly. "I'm sorry about Melanie."

He closed his eyes. "Thanks."

They stood in an uncomfortable silence. "I, well, I went to church this morning in memory of her."

He glanced at her strangely, almost as if he might be angered.

"I didn't know what else to do."

"Thanks for coming," he said. "I didn't know who else to call."

Joanna nodded. "It's okay." Maybe she should change the subject. "You sure are sunburned."

He touched his red face gingerly. "Yeah. It was good sailing until we got the phone call at Catalina. We left right away this morning. So here I am now, and there's nothing I can do." His voice faltered. "I tried to help her. I honestly tried."

She remembered watching from the school bus Friday as he'd talked to Melanie in his car. Then later, during her party, he'd disappeared with her for a long time.

"You want to walk along the beach?" he asked. "I locked up the house."

"Sure." She felt uneasy, unsure of what might happen.

They headed out over the sandy hillside and down toward the ocean. It was November, so there were few people out on the beach. Occasional fierce gusts lifted the dry sand, whipping it through the air, stinging her legs.

Turning to him, she saw Matt's chin trembling. She looked away quickly at the bright blue Pacific.

Great waves gathered in the distance and roared in on the beach, crashing across the sand, foaming at their feet. For a long time they walked the beach in silence. The rushing waves and the surging sound of the ocean made her feel calmer.

"Thanks for coming over," he finally said. "I don't know. I can't seem to talk to the guys about . . . about Melanie. Most of them only saw the wild side of her. You know, I really—" He stopped, gulping.

Was he going to say that he had really loved Melanie? Joanna wondered.

"The guys would figure I got her pregnant," he blurted. "That's what they thought last time. That's what her family thought at first, too."

Melanie had been pregnant . . . and people thought that Matt . . .

Trying to hide her shock, Joanna glanced away at

the ocean. What did Matt mean, *That's what they thought last time*?

It took a while for Joanna to get her courage up. "Was it the second time she was pregnant?"

"Yeah. The second time." He looked far away, up the coast. "She swore she'd never have another abortion. The first one almost drove her crazy. She had terrible nightmares."

Joanna was appalled. A few girls in her high school in Kansas had gotten pregnant, although no one she'd known very well. But twice! Melanie had been pregnant twice!

Matt's words were dull, as if something in him had gone dead, too. "She swore she'd never have another abortion, then she was going to have to . . . again."

No wonder Melanie acted so cold, Joanna thought. She'd been miserably unhappy.

"I drove her to a clinic for the first one last summer," Matt said. "Her mother is always gone to Europe or Arrowhead or some stupid place. She doesn't care about Melanie."

"Matt, were you . . . were you the father?"

"No!" His eyes darkened with despair.

Suddenly he sobbed and sank down on the sand. "I wasn't, but I told her I'd marry her . . . that she could get a divorce from me if that rotten golf pro would marry her later."

"Marry her? But why would you marry her if you weren't the father?" She'd no more than asked than she knew the answer. Because Matt loved Melanie. No matter what else he might say, it was because he loved her.

His body shook as he sat on the sand. "Because . . ." He could hardly force out the words. "Because I feel so guilty, so terribly guilty. When we were younger, I . . . oh, you know. . . ." He closed his eyes and grabbed a

deep breath. "I feel like I got her started . . . I made her
. . . promiscuous."

Joanna couldn't believe this was happening. Matt
had offered to marry Melanie and she'd killed herself
instead. "But why did she kill herself? Something could
have been worked out. Maybe she'd have gotten over
him."

"That was only one part of it," he said, looking
away. "The nightmares were driving her crazy. It got so
she was afraid to sleep. She just couldn't stand them
anymore."

Joanna remembered the hint of dark shadows under
Melanie's eyes. "What kinds of nightmares?"

"Babies. She dreamed about babies. They called her
Mommy, and they reached out to her . . . the first one,
and now this one, too. They'd just be coming to her
when she'd realize they were dead."

Joanna shuddered.

Matt's eyes filled with anguish. "Her shrink said it
was from guilt."

He made himself go on. "She just couldn't take it
anymore. I should have guessed what she might do, but
I didn't want to think about it, and I went sailing! Sailing! And Melanie was killing herself." Tears welled in
his eyes and slid down his cheeks.

Joanna dug in her handbag for tissues and handed
one to him. He shook with silent sobs, and she was
grateful no one was near them, that it was November,
not summer on the beach.

If only I'd shown him the note, she thought. She
wanted to tell him but couldn't say it.

He finally stopped shaking and blew his nose. "I'm
sorry, Joanna, I hardly even know you, but there's no
one else I can talk to. There's no sense in talking to my
father. He wouldn't care. And my mother is so busy

with her new husband and their grand Palm Springs social life."

"It's okay, Matt. I'm glad you thought of me." She wanted to put her arms around him, to protect him.

He tried to smile at her but botched it. "I guess I was interested in you because you looked so sweet, so innocent. It was different for a change."

"Oh, Matt!" she cried, then somehow she was in his arms.

"Please help me," he said, trembling. "Help me, Joanna, please!"

She kissed his forehead, then patted his back gently in the warm sun, as if he were a small child. For a long time they just held each other until he stopped shaking.

At last he looked at her with a sad smile. "You're all right."

How lucky Melanie was to have had him propose, Joanna thought as they got up and brushed off the sand. Had Melanie even appreciated Matt's offer? What a terrible mess it all was. Still, she was glad that he'd called her. She watched him reach into his pocket and pull out a pill bottle. "Matt?"

"It's okay," he said, showing her the label. "Prescription."

She felt relieved. So many people took drugs. "Are you sick?"

"They're for my back. I clobbered it playing ball last winter. Basketball. I guess you wouldn't know."

"I knew you were captain of the team last year."

"Yeah. Well, the doctor says I can't play anymore." He popped the two pills into his mouth and swallowed. "Man, when life starts to get rotten, it sure can go downhill faster and faster."

"What happened to your back?"

"I was going for a lay-up shot, and this clown from

Puente High rammed me—just rammed me. They had to haul me off in an ambulance. Six hours later I came to in the hospital. I was all right except for my stupid back. The doctor says I'm stuck with it."

"I'm sorry, Matt. I'm really sorry."

He got up. "Yeah. Well, it hurts only when I overdo it. It was rough, sailing home this morning." He looked out at the ocean. "Let's forget it."

It did seem that everything in his life was going wrong, but she could make it up to him.

"Listen, I'm sorry for getting choked up on you," he said. "I hope you won't say anything."

"Oh no, Matt! I'd never tell anyone!"

He put an arm around her shoulder as they started back. "You're okay, Joanna."

She smiled at him. "If only I could help you."

"You have. You already have by just listening."

His sad smile made her feel as if she were melting. If only time would stop, right here on the beach, with Matt.

Later, as they walked to his house she said, "There's only one thing that really bothers me, Matt. Friday night at her party you and Melanie disappeared for a long time. When you came back with brambles on your pants, I didn't know what to think."

His sunburned face turned even redder. "I never even thought how that might look. It's a long story." They wandered on as he collected his thoughts. "You see, Melanie was expecting Russ—her fiancé, as she called him, although I don't think he ever planned to marry her. He had other girlfriends, too."

"Was he the father both times?"

"Yeah. Big-deal golf pro. He lived here for a few months. He was Melanie's mother's boyfriend. I guess it must sound crazy to you."

She nodded. "Like something out of a movie, the kind of thing I never thought really happened."

"Anyhow, Melanie and her mother didn't get along. I think her mother was jealous of Melanie being young. And Melanie stole Russ from her mother. Actually her mother probably never knew until later. She left for France last summer . . . when Melanie was pregnant."

"But twice . . . How could Melanie let it happen twice?"

Matt shook his head. "I told her to stay away from Russ after the first time, but she called him right away again. She could have had almost any guy in town, but she had to have one who didn't love her."

It was easy to imagine Melanie's wanting whoever was hardest to get. "But what about her grandparents? Didn't they try to stop her?"

"They tried, but once Melanie had her mind on something nothing could stop her. She was modeling in L.A., and she moved in with him last June. She said she was on the pill, but she got pregnant anyhow. She hadn't told Russ this time. I was supposed to take her to the doctor for another abortion."

"It must have been awful for you!"

"Yeah." He kicked the sand. "It was awful all right. Worst of all, it didn't even stop Melanie. She would have moved right back to L.A. with him. In the meantime, though, another girl moved in with him when school started."

"How could she still love him?" she asked. "I just don't see how!"

"The harder he was to get, the more of a challenge it was for her," Matt answered. "Maybe it's because all her life she had everything she wanted."

Joanna felt like crying for Melanie, for Matt, for the whole awful mess. "Didn't she tell her mom?"

"Yeah, she told her. She thought there might be a way to get him to marry her. But her mother just laughed. She said that Melanie was a stupid fool, that Russ would never get married, that she had to understand men like him. Her mother thought it was an amusing lesson for Melanie."

Matt took a deep breath. "Melanie said she'd prove that Russ loved her. She insisted he'd marry her, and she was so sure of it that she had talked him into coming for her party. She was going to prove to her mother and me and everyone else how much he loved her. Well, he didn't show."

No wonder Melanie had been so cold to her, Joanna thought.

Matt glanced away, embarrassed. "I can imagine what you thought when Melanie and I disappeared at her party. But she was crying and wild and took off down the hillside. I tried to catch her before she threw herself down a bank or something else crazy. I finally got her calmed down. She told me to shut down the party and she'd go to bed."

"So that's when you came back and told everyone to have the last drink?"

He nodded. "That was the end of the party. In more ways than one."

As they climbed up the sandy bank to Matt's house, Joanna wondered what would happen now. He'd called her so he could unload his problems, and he'd sure done it.

"Listen, Joanna," he said, "I really want to make a clean break from the whole mess. That's why I picked you up for school Friday. And that's why I invited you to Melanie's party."

"What do you mean, a clean break?"

He put his arm around her shoulders, and her heart leaped with hope.

"I need another favor."

"Sure. Anything."

"Well, I was wondering if you'd go to her funeral with me. I'd feel a lot better if you were along."

"To Melanie's funeral?"

"Yeah." He looked scared. "It's tomorrow afternoon."

"But I've never been to a funeral. I wouldn't know what to do or say."

"I have to go to it, Joanna." His eyes pleaded. "You'd only have to be there with me."

He looked so pathetic that she knew she'd have to go. "Okay," she decided.

As they walked up through the sand to his driveway, a white Jaguar pulled up, a man and a redheaded young woman in it.

"It's my dad," Matt said.

"Is that his girlfriend?" Joanna asked. The redhead was much younger than Matt's father, maybe just over twenty.

"One of 'em," Matt answered unhappily. "Only one of 'em."

Matt's father climbed out of the Jaguar. "Hey, Matt, what's with Melanie? There were rumors at the club-house."

"I'd better tell you alone," he said. He nodded toward the redhead, who was letting herself out of the car. Both she and Matt's father had joints in their hands, and they looked slightly stoned.

Was that why Matt had passed up the pot at Melanie's party? Because his father was on it? It felt like a long time before Matt introduced them; then there wasn't much to say.

"Guess I'd better be going home. It was nice meeting you," she said to Matt's father and his date.

His father nodded, his eyes glazed. "My pleasure entirely."

"Yeah," his date said. "Nice to meet ya."

"I'll walk you to your car," Matt told Joanna. He looked as if he didn't feel much like telling his father about Melanie.

As she slid into the driver's seat of the Buick, Matt said, "The funeral's at one tomorrow afternoon."

She started the motor, wishing she hadn't agreed to go with him. "Guess we'll have to take the afternoon off from school."

"You really are a friend," he said.

She forced a smile, hoping he couldn't see her disappointment. If there was one thing she didn't want to be to Matt, it was only a friend.

7

The next morning Heidi looked up anxiously from her school bus seat as Joanna joined her. "Did you hear about Melanie?" Heidi whispered, upset. "We were gone for the weekend, and there was a message on our answering machine about the funeral."

Joanna nodded, already dreading the day. Everyone would be talking about Melanie. The funeral this afternoon at one o'clock seemed way too soon. It was as if Melanie's family wanted to get it over with quickly. She smoothed her navy blue dress under her, having worn it so she and Matt could leave for the funeral from school.

"You were at Melanie's party Friday night," Heidi said. "What happened?"

"It didn't happen until after the party," Joanna answered, trying not to think of the note.

"Melanie was wild," Heidi explained, "but I didn't expect she'd ever kill herself."

Joanna noticed that the two sophomore girls sitting behind them were leaning forward, listening intently. She glanced away, but not quickly enough.

"Why did Melanie do it?" one of them asked. "I heard she was pregnant."

"No," Joanna lied, deciding it was none of their business. "No, she wasn't."

"She must have been on drugs," the other girl remarked. "After all, she OD'd on sleeping pills."

Joanna shrugged and looked away.

Heidi waited until the sophomores had settled back into their seats. "I heard she was crazy about an older guy in L.A., but he wasn't quite as crazy about her." She thought for a moment. "Still, I couldn't see her copping out over that. She was always so tough. I can't imagine anything making her do it."

Joanna wished the day were over already or that Matt hadn't told her about Melanie's nightmares. In her mind's eye Joanna saw little babies reaching out. She shivered.

"Will you be going to the funeral?" Heidi asked.

Joanna nodded, looking blindly past her out the bus window.

"You could go with me and my family," Heidi offered. "My parents have known the Tillinghasts for years, so they're going. My dad is her—the grandparents' doctor."

"Thanks, but I'm going with Matt."

Heidi looked at her in surprise. "Oh."

Miserable as the whole mess was, Joanna thought, the words "I'm going with Matt" had a special ring to them. Even Heidi looked at her with a kind of respect. It would be interesting to hear what everyone would say about their being together at Melanie's funeral.

Later, as they were getting off the school bus, Joanna was glad to see Matt waiting for her at the bus door. She almost tripped down the steps in nervousness.

He caught her arm and steadied her. "Clumsy," he said with a small grin that quickly faded.

"You scared me with that bright red face," she answered, just to say something. Actually, his sunburn was already turning into a wonderful tan, and his sun-bleached hair shimmered in the morning sunshine. His sadness, she thought, made him look even more appealing.

She recalled the warmth of his hand on her arm to steady her and wished he would hold her hand now. After a moment she said, "You didn't wear your dark suit." He was wearing navy blue pants and a short-sleeved white shirt, open at the collar. He'd said he would wear a dark suit to school.

He blinked in confusion. "Oh. Oh, yeah."

Was he on those pain pills this morning? She decided not to ask, surrounded as they were with people getting off the yellow school buses and everyone looking at them.

As they started up the leaf-covered steps to the school, she wondered why he'd met her at the school bus. Did he want to somehow separate himself from Melanie in people's minds? Did he want everyone to think that he'd already been interested in Joanna Stevens?

Chad met them in front of the American lit. classroom, looking subdued. "You going to the funeral?" he asked Matt. "There's a lot of us going together."

Matt considered Chad's offer for a moment. "Thanks," he replied, "but I'm taking Joanna."

"Yeah?" Chad asked, surprised. He gave her an appreciative glance. "Well, we might not actually make it there anyway. It's not our first choice for a great afternoon."

"You better go!" Matt said with vehemence, then turned abruptly to Joanna. "See you at twelve by the parking lot."

The classroom buzzed with talk about Melanie, and Mrs. Ekelman did not arrive until long after the bell. There'd been a faculty meeting, she explained. She looked down at her desk, then finally up at them. "I'm sorry to have to tell you that Melanie Tillinghast died early Saturday morning. Those of you who wish to go to the funeral this afternoon will be excused."

The class was uncomfortably quiet.

"Now, if you'll turn to page . . ."

Mrs. Ekelman looked pale, as if she shared in the fault, too.

All morning everyone talked about Melanie. Even freshmen gathered in small groups that dispersed too quickly and quietly. Solemn twosomes and threesomes of teachers whispered to each other. It made Joanna's own guilt even worse.

At noon she rushed down to the parking lot and found Matt already waiting in the red Corvette. "Have you been waiting long?" she asked.

"A while." He leaned across the seat to open her door. "I couldn't make it through the last class, so I've been sitting out here."

Their eyes met, his turned away first. "Felt like everyone was watching me."

"You're just imagining it, Matt. Why should they watch you?"

"Yeah," he said absently. "Well, let's go. We have to stop at my house for my jacket. I don't know—I can't seem to keep my mind on track. I'm forgetting everything."

"I'll keep an eye on you, okay?" she promised, and he gave her an appreciative nod. She loved him, she thought. She really did.

She was glad when they pulled out of the parking lot and he turned on the radio. It seemed wrong to love anyone when Melanie was just barely dead. Why did life go on for the rest of them?

"I couldn't get through this without you," he said.

"I've only been to my grandparents' funerals."

"We'll get through it." Despite the sinking feeling below her ribs, her voice was firm. She didn't know how *she* was going to make it through either.

By the time they picked up Matt's jacket and drove over to the southern colonial-style funeral home it was twelve-thirty. The parking lot adjoining the funeral home was filling up rapidly with Melanie's family, neighbors, and friends. Matt looked solemn as he nodded and waved. He seemed to know almost everyone there, and Joanna saw them staring frankly at her.

Chad cruised past them with his van full of friends.

Matt was delaying, taking forever to close up the car, comb his hair, put on his jacket. "Well, we'd better go in," he finally said. He took out his pills.

She frowned as he put one into his mouth. "Is your back hurting?"

He swallowed the pill. "Headache."

They started toward the funeral home reluctantly.

A somber man in a black suit met them at the front door. "Melanie Tillinghast?"

When they nodded, he handed them white cards.

"In Memoriam," the cards said. "Melanie Anne Tillinghast."

"The Blue Room," the man said. He motioned them to a door from which soft organ music sounded.

Ahead of them others stood signing the guest book, and they followed them through the overpowering perfume of flowers. Joanna caught her breath, trying not to gag on the sickly sweet smell. *Should have eaten today,* she thought. Moments later they stepped into the rear of the large Blue Room. It felt as if she were walking into another world, she thought, then it occurred to her that she was. She was walking into the realm of the dead.

Mourners sat on row upon row of folding chairs; flowers lined the front and side walls of the room.

Joanna's eyes traveled forward and stopped. Melanie's casket. She must have been staring too long because Matt's hand was on her elbow.

"You okay?" he whispered. "Your face is white."

She swallowed hard and nodded, starting forward with the line of people before she realized where they were heading. Each person walked to the casket, then slowly, one by one, looked at Melanie.

Joanna glanced around quickly. No way to escape. She and Matt would have to go, too.

Joanna kept her eyes on the flowers as they moved forward, hoping she wouldn't faint. "We should have sent flowers," she whispered to Matt, who looked paralyzed himself.

"Dad sent some. And the senior class sent a plant."

"Is your father coming?"

He shook his head. "No way. He doesn't get involved."

"Are you okay?"

"I don't know," he answered, "but I'm going to make it."

Suddenly they were at the front of the line, and it was her turn to pass by the casket. She felt chilled as she forced herself to look. Melanie wore a white dress, and her face was nearly as white as the dress. Her dark hair lay spread across a pillow, but she didn't look as if she were sleeping, Joanna thought. Instead, she looked empty, as if she were made of wax. The bottom half of the casket was closed, covered with a blanket of pink rosebuds. They had tried to make Melanie look sweet and innocent, a sleeping princess.

She felt Matt's arm at her elbow again, and she moved on past the casket and to the rows of chairs, softly gasping for breath. If only they could sit down. She saw empty chairs next to Heidi and concentrated hard on getting there.

Heidi was patting her arm. "You all right?"

Joanna shook her head as if she were awakening from a dream. "I think so." She looked around for Matt and saw him shaking hands with people in the front row.

"Who's that?" She nodded at the slim, elegant woman in a powder blue dress talking to Matt.

"Melanie's mother," Heidi said. "And those are her grandparents."

The elderly couple now shaking hands with Matt were as slim and elegant as Melanie's mother.

Joanna had thought that someone in the family might be crying, but everyone seemed composed and dry eyed.

"They're holding up very well," Heidi remarked. "At least that's what everyone is saying."

It sounded like a compliment, Joanna thought, but somehow, if she were dead in that white satin-lined casket, she hoped someone would cry.

Matt headed down the aisle toward her, then he sat down stiffly. "They're going to have her cremated," he whispered, sounding as if he could hardly believe it. "They're going to burn her."

Joanna closed her eyes, unwilling to think about it. She'd pretend she hadn't heard him. After a moment, she glanced sideways at him.

He was shaking with silent sobs, trying to open his white memorial card.

She turned away to keep from breaking down. Opening her memorial card, she stared at Melanie's birth and death dates. Below them, it said:

The Lord is my shepherd: I shall not want.

He maketh me to lie down in green pastures: he leadeth me beside the still waters.

He restoreth my soul: he leadeth me in the paths of righteousness for his name's sake.

Yea, though I walk through the valley of the shadow of death, I will fear no evil: for thou art with me: thy rod and thy staff they comfort me.

Thou preparest a table before me in the presence of mine enemies: thou anointest my head with oil: my cup runneth over.

Surely goodness and mercy shall follow me all the days of my life: And I will dwell in the house of the Lord for ever.

Psalm 23

It didn't make sense. No matter how beautiful it sounded, how could it apply to Melanie? She'd walked in a shadow of death and swallowed a bottleful of sleeping pills. God hadn't helped her. And surely she wouldn't dwell in the house of the Lord forever. If there was any life after death, her soul was probably on fire!

The murmur of the crowd grew, almost drowning out the soft organ music. Old friends greeted one another. A short line of mourners formed to speak to Melanie's family, and David and some of his friends filed by the casket.

Chad and eight or nine others from school came in and sat down two rows behind them without passing the casket. Joanna wished she hadn't passed the casket either.

It seemed hours before Gary, the young minister, stepped forward to the lectern microphone. "We are gathered here today . . ." he began, and the words whirled around Joanna without any meaning. He said something about God's forgiving anything if we come to Him; that we have love and forgiveness through His only begotten Son, Jesus Christ; that God is love, and He forgives us for caving in to the pressures of this world.

After a while, she realized that heads were bowed in prayer.

"We entrust her into your hands," Gary prayed, "and we ask that we learn to be more sensitive, more caring to people all around us."

Joanna saw Melanie's crumpled note in her mind's eye again: "I don't want to go on. . . . I can't do it again."

"Are you all right?" Heidi asked, helping Joanna up.

She saw that her row was standing, starting up to the casket. *Now what?* she wondered, glancing at Matt.

He was biting his lips hard, but tears streamed down his cheeks. He blotted them with his folded handkerchief. "I can't make it," he whispered. "I can't make it."

They were next to move forward.

"Concentrate on the flowers."

He grabbed her elbow with a painful grip, and they moved slowly forward until they were at the casket again. She couldn't concentrate on the flowers. Instead, her eyes moved to the white waxen shell of Melanie. She'd never forget this day.

Matt pushed her elbow, then they were trying not to rush from the pale blue room too fast. They made it to the vestibule, then to the front door. . . .

Hot wind and sunshine washed over Joanna, and she stood, breathing in the fresh air. Slowly she became aware of the long black limousine waiting for Melanie's family.

Matt grabbed her hand. "Come on, I have to get away from here!"

"It's over, Matt," she said, pulling him back to a fast walk. "People are looking at you. It's over."

His eyes were dry when they reached his car. "Not for me, it's not over." He stared briefly at the black limousine behind them again. "It's never going to be over!"

He sounded a little wild. "You want me to drive?" she asked.

"No." For a long time he just sat in the car, not turning on the ignition, just staring. He wasn't seeing anything in particular, she realized. His mind was flipping through the past, looking at memories of Melanie.

"Come on, Matt, I'll drive!"

He shook his head, as if realizing where he was, then started the car. "We're going to Melanie's house. Her mother is expecting all of us there."

"You're kidding!"

"No. It's customary," he said, his voice numb. "They'll probably have a bar and ham and cheeses. All of that. Everybody does it, I guess."

"I can't believe that people would have a—a party."

"That's what they do," he said.

Chad's van pulled out onto the street.

"Are Chad and the rest of them going?" she asked.

"I guess so. They've all known her since we were kids, too."

They pulled out of the parking lot and followed Chad's van onto the main road. "Part of life," Matt remarked. "That's what my dad said anyhow. Dying's part of life. . . ."

Then why hadn't his father come to the funeral if dying was part of life? Joanna wanted to ask. She turned on the radio to the rock station and tried to keep her mind on the music. Maybe music had a more predictable beat than life.

Later, pulling up to the gatehouse at Santa Rosita Hills, she recalled Friday night when she had first come here. It had been night, but everything had sparkled with bright excitement. Now the sun beamed on them, and life felt hideously dark.

The uniformed guard stepped forward. "Good afternoon, Matt."

Matt was unsmiling now. "Hi, Hank. We're going to the Tillinghasts'."

"I was sorry to hear about it," the guard said, then punched the button to open the road gate.

Inside the gate Joanna looked at the rolling hillsides of orange and lemon groves and the acres of white-fenced horse pastures. There were horseback riders on the trails, riding along in the hot wind as if nothing unpleasant had happened in the world. In the distance, large houses sprawled across hilltops. It was unreal, she thought. As unreal as the last four days had been. When would life ever get back to normal? It seemed that everything had gone wrong with the coming of the Santa Ana winds. They were devil winds, all right. She wondered if David and his church friends called them that.

"You're quiet," Matt remarked.

"You too."

"Do you suppose we'll ever get over this?" he asked, his lips trembling.

"Maybe—maybe after a while," she replied, unsure.

He pulled up into the Tillinghast driveway. "Melanie doesn't live here anymore," he said, his voice shaking. He steered the car into a narrow parking space between cars and turned off the ignition. Reaching into his suit pocket, he pulled out his pill vial.

"Is your back still hurting?" she asked.

"Don't nag." He sat with a pill in his hand for a moment, then popped it into his mouth and swallowed hard. "Come on, let's go in. I want to get this over with."

She was glad he grabbed her hand and held it tightly

as they walked up the driveway. Even while they waited for Chad and the others to unload from their cars, Matt held on to her hand. He was holding it when they walked up to the house and through its wide-open double doors.

"The bar's outside," someone said.

They walked through the long Tudor living room with a stone fireplace that covered most of the far wall, then outside again through the open French doors. The patio, bright with flowers, had tables and chairs around the pool, just as it'd been for Melanie's party. Her family was not in sight.

Matt held her hand all the way to the bar. "Double scotch," he said to Juan, then turned to Joanna, waiting for her order.

"Just white wine, I guess."

Matt gulped his drink down. "Awful," he said to Juan with a grimace. "I'll have another one."

Joanna felt her stomach churn. Matt sounded almost like her father! She glanced at him standing next to her, blond hair glistening in the sunshine. No, he was nothing like her father. Matt was special, like no one she'd ever known before.

She and Matt were on their next drink when they sat down with Chad and the others.

"I got started on the booze right outside that funeral home," Chad said. "That's the only way I could get myself in there."

Time swirled around them like the sunshine. It seemed hours later when Melanie's grandparents stopped by to thank them for coming. "Now don't be shy about eating," Mr. Tillinghast said. "The food is in the dining room."

"We'd better eat something," Chad said. "I'm barely standing."

It looked as though Chad were afloat. His eyes seemed unfocused. She hoped that he didn't intend to chase her across the yard again as he had Friday night.

"Aren't you reeling yet?" he asked her. "You're sure putting that wine away."

"Let's have something to eat," she told Matt.

In the dining room, a long table was laden with mounds of sliced ham, turkey, roast beef, and cheeses. Next came trays of breads and rolls; potato salad, cole-slaw, crab salad. A buffet held rich cakes, pies, cookies, and expensive chocolates.

"I haven't eaten all day," she remembered.

"You have to be home for dinner?" Matt asked.

"I told Mom I'd probably be late. Maybe I'd better call anyway." An uneasy thought about her dad skittered through her head. She glanced at the door into the kitchen. A woman was using the phone. "I'll call later," she said, and followed Matt with her plate of food to the tables on the far side of the patio.

Chad and the others gathered around with their plates of food, and Juan brought over glasses and two bottles of Italian white wine. Later Melanie's elegant mother stopped by. "It's so kind of all of you to come over," she said with a wan smile, then moved on, stopping to say a few gracious words to everyone.

She was very lovely, Joanna thought. Melanie would have looked like her someday.

It was eleven o'clock before they realized how late it was for a school night. Joanna stood up and tottered. She looked at Matt. He staggered even more.

He was laughing at himself as he stumbled about, then flopped down hard on a chair. "We really got bombed," he said, holding his head. "Well, it was in honor of Melanie. . . ." He was suddenly sobbing.

"Come on, Matt," Joanna urged, trying to tug him to his feet.

"Okay, Matt," Chad said, grabbing him under an arm. "Looks like this time I drive you home. You can leave your wheels here."

Joanna lifted Matt's other arm over her shoulder, and they began to stagger out together with him.

"Bye! Thanks!" Chad yelled for all of them as they started for the darkness around the side yard.

"Afraid we're not making such a good impression on our elders," one of the girls remarked.

"Most of them are stoned or drunk themselves," someone muttered.

They glanced at a group of adults, who stared at them with disapproval.

"We did it for Melanie!" Matt shouted at them so loudly that everyone turned. "And don't any of you ever forget her!"

Everyone was suddenly quiet, looking at him. The silence held all the way down the driveway except for Matt's yelling, "We . . . did it for Melanie . . . for Melanie!"

Joanna's heart ached.

"It's getting cold," someone said, and Joanna realized the Santa Ana winds had stopped.

8

As Chad drove his van up her driveway, Joanna saw the outdoor lights on. The crowd in the van was singing a raucous song at the top of their voices. "Quiet, please be quiet!" she pleaded, but everyone only acted crazier. Matt sang even louder than the rest. "Please, Matt, I'll get in trouble."

He tried to stand up as the van stopped. "Wake up, neighborhood! Joanna's home!" he shouted drunkenly.

"Thanks. Thanks a lot," she told him as she got out. She slid the van door shut quickly, grateful at least that its windows were closed as everyone yelled good-night. She rushed to the house, thinking that she'd have to act sober if her mother were up.

The front door opened, and Joanna caught her breath. Her mother stood at the door.

"Hi, Mom."

"Are you all right?" her mother asked, letting Joanna in. "It's so late for a Monday night. I thought you'd at least call." As she closed the door, her eyes widened. "Have you been drinking, Joanna?"

"Just some Italian wine at the Tillinghasts', Mom. Not much."

"Not much?" her mother echoed, following her through the entry. "You reek of it!"

Joanna stopped, frightened by her mother's anger.

"How could you do it! How could you!" Mom's face

was white. "I just got your drunken father home from the police station and put him to bed. And now you!"

Joanna's head cleared quickly. "The police station! What happened to Dad?"

"He's been drinking since Saturday night, that's what. He hasn't been home for two days." Tears burst from her eyes. "Here I am trying to protect you girls from reality, and you come home drunk!"

Joanna hugged her mother. "I'm sorry, Mom. I didn't know. I . . . I thought I saw Dad Sunday on the way to Matt's."

"Where?"

"By those awful bars on the Coast Highway."

"Why didn't you call me?" her mother demanded.

Joanna shook her head. "I just didn't think it could be him."

"Well, it was," Mom said. "Now I have to sober him up for work tomorrow. He didn't make it to the office today, and I had to lie for him again."

"Is he okay now?"

"He's wretched. But he'll probably be all right in the morning."

"I'm sorry, Mom." She wished she could explain how truly sorry she was.

"I don't need another drunk in this family!"

"It was the funeral," Joanna protested. "It was hideous. Then the Tillinghasts insisted that we come over, and we didn't eat properly all day. All I drank was white wine."

"Thank goodness for that," her mother said. She looked away for a moment. "I'm afraid that if this happens again, we're going to have to send your father to a hospital or a clinic."

"Oh, Mom," Joanna said in agony.

"Well, I have to get to bed. I'm exhausted," her mother said.

"Good-night, Mom. I love you."

Her mother turned with a weary smile. "Night, dear. I love you, too."

How could her father do this to them? Joanna wondered on the way to her room. She hoped Cathy would never find out. What if everyone in school learned that their father had been drunk at the Santa Rosita police station?

She quickly undressed for bed. She could still see Melanie in her casket . . . Matt staggering down the driveway at the Tillinghasts' house . . . her mother so upset. . . . Even in bed she couldn't stop the memories.

She was feeling nervous and jumpy. Recalling that her mother kept tranquilizers in a kitchen cabinet, Joanna crawled out of bed. She felt her way through the dark house. In the kitchen she turned on the range light, found the pill bottles, and took two of the tiny tranquilizers.

Maybe she should take a bottle of sherry to her room, just in case she couldn't get to sleep anyhow. She climbed up onto the kitchen counter and looked through the liquor bottles. Two full bottles of sherry.

Taking one out carefully, she carried it to her room and hid it in the back of her closet. She'd have it later if she couldn't get to sleep. She'd keep it there, just in case.

———

The next day Matt arrived at school at noon. He looked terrible, Joanna thought as he came over to her locker, but then she didn't feel so good either. When she'd gotten up this morning, she'd taken aspirin and antacid tablets and used eye drops for her bloodshot eyes.

Everyone at school seemed subdued. The only good thing all day was that Matt walked her to her classes and drove her home. The next morning his red Corvette was at her front door when she started out for the school bus.

It became a wonderful life, Matt driving her to school and home, walking at her side between classes. Their names were coupled everywhere: Matt and Joanna . . . Joanna and Matt. Other students looked at her with respect. Joanna Stevens had risen from nobody to Matt Thompson's girl!

At home, family life seemed better. Her father was quiet, bringing work home from his office and taking it to the den with him every evening. Her mother looked happier. And Cathy didn't seem to know anything had been wrong. She was more interested in finding out about her new idol, Matt.

"Did Matt kiss you yet?" Cathy asked the next Saturday afternoon as they cleaned house.

Joanna smiled and turned on the vacuum cleaner. Matt still hadn't tried to kiss her. Last night—Friday— a whole crowd of them had gone to a movie. Matt had put his arm around the back of her seat, barely touching her shoulder, and that was all.

Anyhow, it had been an odd evening. After the movie they'd had a few drinks at the beach in Chad's van, then went home early. The boys were going sailing at six the next morning.

As she vacuumed the house, Joanna hoped that they'd be in early from sailing, especially since Matt had asked her to meet him at his house. She'd much rather have him pick her up, but he'd already looked impatient when she asked what they were going to do.

He did not like being pushed.

That evening as she pulled up in her mother's minivan at Matt's house, Chad's van was just leaving. She was glad to see Chad wave and drive on.

Matt ambled to her car, sunburned again and grinning. "Thanks for driving," he said, opening the car door for her. "I'm beat."

He did look tired.

"Would you mind just watching TV?" he asked, looking a little embarrassed.

"Of course not." The truth was she didn't care what they did as long as they were together. She looked up at him, wishing he'd kiss her now, right here on the driveway. She didn't care who saw them.

"I have to clean up. You want to wait inside? Rena's there . . . and Dad."

She did not feel like making polite conversation with anyone. "I'll take a walk on the beach, okay?"

"Sure. I'll hurry."

She smiled as he rushed for the house.

Pulling off her sneakers, she threw them into the minivan, then headed slowly down the bank to the sandy beach. The ocean was silvery blue, reflecting the clouds. It would be a beautiful sunset, she thought, hoping Matt would be with her to enjoy it. She didn't like being alone anymore with so many unpleasant thoughts to crowd in. There was just too much she didn't want to remember.

She stood for a long moment, lost in the vastness of the surging ocean. Crashing waves drowned out the world as she walked down the hard, wet sand, then stood waiting for water to lap at her feet. Suddenly foaming cold water rushed at her, swirling around her ankles, and she backed away before the next wave raced across the sand at her.

Turning to walk along the shore, she wondered if she could walk to Alaska along the coast. Sure, there were rivers and cliffs, but it didn't seem like it from here. Maybe someday she and Matt could just walk away, far away, along the ocean's edge. It was a crazy idea, like in old movies when someone walked into the sunset.

"Joanna!"

A blond woman, her hair encased in a filmy scarf, waved as she hurried to catch up with her.

Rena . . . it was Rena. How much younger she always looked as she came closer. She had such a joyous smile and luminous eyes.

"I was hoping to talk to you. May I?"

"Sure," Joanna said, then waited until Rena fell in step with her. What could she want to discuss?

"Isn't it beautiful here?" Rena asked.

Joanna nodded, certain that Rena wanted to talk about more than the scenery.

"I try to walk here every day, and still I'm overwhelmed by the beauty of the ocean and the sky," Rena remarked.

"It must be wonderful to live here, by the ocean."

"Sometimes," Rena answered. "But a lot of people don't really see the ocean, even when they live next to it. Living here doesn't seem to make life free of problems."

Joanna wondered if Rena was going to mention something about Matt's drinking or taking too many pills. "Is something wrong?" Joanna finally asked.

"Yes, something is very wrong, and I'm hoping you can help Matt. He's in for bad news."

Joanna bit her lip. *Now what?*

"It's money problems," Rena said. "His father has had financial reverses in his business. He's going to put the house up for sale. And the sailboat, too."

"Oh no!"

"Matt's been through so much lately," Rena explained. "I try to talk to him, but he's only known me for a few months . . . and I'm only around part time. He needs someone to understand him, to help him now." Her eyes pleaded. "You will help him, won't you?"

"I'll try," Joanna promised. But how could she help Matt with this?

She stopped and turned to go back to Matt's house.

"Thank you," Rena said gratefully. "I'll pray for you."

Pray for me! Joanna thought. What right did anyone have to pray for someone who didn't want it?

"God bless you, dear." Rena threw a little kiss and started off.

Joanna felt helpless as she watched the woman continue down the beach. She meant well, but . . . she wished she hadn't heard a word Rena had said. Especially right here on the beach where Matt had been so upset about Melanie.

The sun slipped behind a cloud, and a sudden cold wind whipped across the ocean.

Joanna shivered and started back, wondering what Matt would do now.

Nearing the house, she saw Matt's father leaving with a young woman in his white Jaguar. She wasn't sure whether they saw her or not. If they did, they purposely ignored her.

She walked up the sandy incline to the enclosed patio and unlatched the wooden gate. Inside, a wall of glass windows shielded her from the ocean wind. She sank down on a chaise lounge.

A moment later she saw Matt heading out to look for her on the beach. "I'm in here, Matt."

How glum he looked, she thought as he walked toward the enclosed patio. "The wind was getting too cold," she said as he let himself in the side gate.

He slammed the gate shut and threw himself down on the other lounge.

"Is something wrong?"

"Just about everything," he replied.

She didn't know what to say. "Do you want to talk about it?"

His eyes avoided hers. "I don't even want to think about it!" It was a while before he continued. "This house is going up for sale."

Joanna tried to look surprised. "I'm sorry, Matt."

"Yeah, me too! First, we sell the house in Santa Rosita Hills, now this one, and he's talking about a small condo."

"Your father must feel terrible about it."

"Who knows?" he asked. "All he seems to care about is young chicks." After a long silence, he added, "Let's go get a drink!"

As she followed him into the house, she expected him to say something about selling the sailboat, but maybe his father hadn't told him that yet.

In the den Matt stopped in front of the bar. "Do you really like me—just me as a person?"

Couldn't he see that she loved him? "Yes, Matt. I like you a lot."

He looked at her for a long time, then leaned down and softly kissed her forehead.

She waited for his arms to close around her, for a real kiss, but he held her lightly by the shoulders. He only liked her. He only liked her, and he still loved Melanie!

"Let's go out for pizza," he said. "We could go to Morelli's."

"Sounds great!" It sounded a lot better than starting to drink with Matt already so upset.

———

All the way to Morelli's and during their pizza and salad dinner, Matt kept Joanna talking about her old life in Kansas, about cheerleading for games, about the crazy things she and her friends had done. She brought out shining memories as if thumbing through her photo album.

As they talked, light from the red candle on their table flickered across their faces. There was a glow all around them, across the red and white checkered tablecloth, and she felt as if Matt were part of the glow when she made him laugh at her memories. Yet it felt, too, as if they were only pretending to be happy.

" . . . and Cappie," she was saying, "Cappie, my best friend since kindergarten . . ." Oh, how she missed Cappie and Sara and Dena and everyone else. She suddenly felt like crying.

Other Santa Rosita High kids were in the dimly lit restaurant. *How happy we must look to them,* Joanna thought. She glanced around at people in the trellised room with its green plastic leaves and reddish grape clusters hanging everywhere. Did others pretend to be happy to hide their hurts? Did everyone see through her smiles to her loneliness in this new school . . . and through Matt's grins to his terrible heartaches? Her throat tightened so that she could scarcely breathe.

Matt looked at her strangely, then excused himself to go to the rest room.

Had he noticed that there was something wrong with her? Did he care?

Moments later David Porter was sliding into Matt's chair. "How's everything going, Joanna?" he asked.

Where did he come from? she wondered, her hand trembling as she reached for her water glass. She nearly tipped it over, but David righted it just in time. "Are you okay?"

"Of course. Why shouldn't I be?" she asked. But her words sounded unconvincing, even to herself.

His eyes were soft with concern. "You sure?"

She nodded, hoping she wouldn't cry.

"Can I pick you up for church tomorrow morning?"

She nodded. Anything to keep from crying here in front of everyone.

"I'll pick you up at nine-thirty." He got up with a glance at the rest rooms. "See you then."

She managed a smile but didn't answer. She wasn't even sure what had happened and glanced around the restaurant to see if David was actually there. Maybe their conversation had been in her imagination, she thought until she saw him heading for a table near the window. There were some of the people who had been at his party. She turned away fast. Why on earth had she agreed to go with him? The last time she went to church she had vowed never to go again!

"Something wrong?" Matt asked when he sat down across from her again.

"No. Not at all."

On their way out of Morelli's, he suggested, "Let's go home and watch TV. There won't be anyone there."

Joanna felt uneasy, not knowing what to expect. "Okay," she finally answered. She could almost feel David looking at her as they left.

At Matt's house they settled down in the den in front of the big color TV. He sprawled out next to her on the brown leather couch with a glass of red wine. What he wanted to do was drink, she decided when he poured himself one drink after another.

"What's wrong, you too good to drink?" he asked her.

"That's not it at all, Matt." She didn't want to tell him about her father.

"You don't like me," Matt said.

"What are you talking about?"

"If you liked me," he said, "you'd drink with me." He grabbed her hand and kissed her fingers, then his kisses moved up her bare arm. Suddenly he pulled away and turned his back to her.

She wanted him to go on, to melt in his arms. She wanted him to kiss her forever. What had gone wrong? "Okay," she finally said, "I'll have some wine."

An hour later she was in his arms, and his kisses thrilled her beyond her imaginings. She wanted to tell him how much she loved him, but he would have to tell her first.

By midnight they were drinking their second bottle of wine. "I have to go home, Matt," she finally said. She stood up and tottered. "Oh no! And I have to drive, too."

"Follow me, my lovely," he said, leading her to the kitchen. "Would you believe that I can make instant coffee? Clever, eh?"

She watched him as he got out a cup and the instant coffee. Lately, every time he tried to be funny, it seemed to be because he was hiding something. "What's wrong, Matt?"

He turned away. "Dad's put the sailboat up for sale! It's been the only thing that makes me forget how rotten my life is now."

She reached her arms up to him. "I'll help you, Matt. I'll make you forget everything, no matter what I have to do."

Matt caught her in his arms, and they held on to each other desperately.

Driving home, she was remembering that moment

when suddenly headlights pierced the blackness and beamed straight at her. Terrified, she whipped the mini-van to the right, barely missing the oncoming lights. The other car roared past her into the night, its horn blaring.

In horror, Joanna gripped the steering wheel with all of her strength as her car's right tires shimmied on the road's gravel shoulder. Finally she slowed the car. Shaking, she pulled off the road and stopped on the gravel. For a long time, she sat in the darkness, picturing those headlights coming straight at her again and again. How could she have strayed over the middle line like that?

She opened the front windows wide for fresh air and recalled her promise to Matt: "I'll make you forget everything, no matter what I have to do."

9

When Joanna awakened the next morning she felt awful. She remembered drinking the red wine at Matt's house, then the coffee so she could drive home. She saw the car's headlights piercing the night, coming at her. When she sat up quickly, her head lurched.

Maybe aspirin would help again. She padded barefoot across the white carpeting to the medicine cabinet in her bathroom, hazily recalling that she was supposed to go somewhere.

Church . . . She'd told David she'd go to church with him!

"Joanna?" Cathy whispered at the door. "Are you up?"

"Come on in. But I have to get dressed."

Cathy stepped in quietly, her eyes downcast.

"What's wrong?" Joanna asked.

"Everything, oh, everything." She grabbed a deep breath, as if she might cry. "Mom and Dad were fighting last night. Mom said she's going to leave if he doesn't stop drinking!"

"Oh, Cathy."

Cathy nodded, looking too wretched for tears.

Reaching out for Cathy, Joanna wondered if her little sister had cried in bed last night. "Cathy, I promised David that I'd go to church with him this morning, but you could go, too. He wouldn't mind at all. We'd have to be ready at nine-thirty."

Cathy looked uncertain. "I'd better ask Mom, and she's not up yet. She's sleeping in the guest room."

"I'll be responsible. Let's just get dressed. You could wear your green velvet dress and your new black patent shoes."

Joanna wondered what her mother would say this time about her going to church . . . and taking Cathy! Yet when their mother got up, she seemed relieved that they were going out. "Have a nice time," she called after them as they left.

It was a strange thing to say when someone was going to church, Joanna thought.

David was pleased to see Cathy as she and Joanna climbed into his car. "Hey, I didn't even think about inviting you. I'm glad you're coming along." He looked as if he meant it. "You could come to church with us, or you could go to Sunday school."

"I guess I'd rather go with you," Cathy said shyly. "I've never been to a church."

David seemed surprised. "Well, then, I'm especially happy that you're going. You can go anytime with me, you know."

How pleased Cathy looked to be included, Joanna thought, feeling better about going. She should include Cathy in more things. Maybe they could go somewhere this afternoon since Matt was sailing. Heidi was always inviting her over to go horseback riding, telling her to bring Cathy along. She could call Heidi when they got home.

The church bells were pealing all around them as the three of them climbed out of David's yellow car.

"It sounds beautiful," Cathy told David.

"I always think so, too," he answered.

Joanna straightened Cathy's collar. At least she could get her mind off her parents' fighting for a while.

Inside the church Cathy's awe grew. Her eyes widened with wonder as she walked down the aisle with Joanna and David amid the soft organ music. She sat down between them. "What if I don't know what to do?"

"Just watch David," Joanna whispered, remembering how uncertain she'd been the first time.

Cathy nodded, then showed Joanna the front of the program. It was bright with autumn leaves, Indian corn, pumpkins, and apples. "The Lord is good to all. Psalm 145:9," it said.

Before long, they were standing and singing "Onward, Christian soldiers, marching as to war . . ." The yellow-robed choir members moved forward by twos down the middle aisle, singing out mightily as they filed past the pews.

How can Christians be soldiers? Joanna wondered. So much about it didn't make sense.

Cathy loved everything. "What a friend we have in Jesus," she sang along with a shy smile.

Joanna turned away to hide the fact that she wasn't singing much.

The minister said, "We pray for the sick, the lonely, the confused, the hurting people of this world. We ask that they might know that Jesus loves them and wants to be their friend."

Joanna suddenly found herself praying. "Oh, God, if you exist, please help my sister, Cathy . . . and please help my mother and father . . . and me, too."

Cathy touched her hand. "Look, it's some kids from my class at school. There's Dede! I didn't know she went to this church!"

White-robed children grouped themselves in front of the altar, then looked uneasily out at the congregation. A woman stepped forward to direct them, then they all smiled, as if on cue.

"Jesus loves the little children," they sang. "All the children of the world. Red and yellow, black and white, they are precious in His sight . . ."

When the song ended and the children filed out, Cathy whispered, "I loved that."

The minister was talking about grace, but Joanna couldn't quite understand. The program said, "For it is by grace you have been saved, through faith—and this not from yourselves, it is the gift of God."

Grace, then, was God's love, she thought. God loved everyone. But it didn't seem possible that He loved murderers and thieves and . . .

The service was coming to an end with "Amazing Grace." The minister had said it was written by a man who had bought and sold slaves. A slave trader!

She tried to understand. "I once was lost but now I'm found, was blind but now I see. . . . How precious did that grace appear the hour I first believed."

How had this man who was a slave trader come to believe in God?

As they stood up to leave, Cathy said, "I never thought church would be like that."

"Like what?" David asked.

"So wonderful," she answered. "I thought it would be boring and dumb, and not so . . . beautiful."

David looked pleased, and Cathy looked so happy, almost as if she had forgotten what had happened last night.

When they drove home, the day seemed full of sunshine.

As they pulled up in their driveway, they heard a scream. Her mother! Joanna glanced at David.

He'd heard, too. "You want me to come in?"

"No, it's just—" She couldn't think what to say, then

remembered something about scream therapy—a show on TV. "It's my mother's scream therapy. You know, to get rid of stress. Thanks anyway, and thanks for taking us."

Cathy's face was ashen. "Thanks, David. I loved your church."

As they hurried in the front door, Joanna heard her parents in the family room.

"Give me those car keys!" her father yelled, twisting her mother's arm to get them from her.

Her lip was bleeding badly. "The girls are here, can't you see that?"

"Dad!" Joanna shouted angrily.

He glanced at her in disgust, and her mother tried to pull away. "You're going to kill yourself, driving in this condition."

He slapped her face hard and pushed her against the family room wall, but with one desperate push she broke his hold. She threw the keys to Joanna.

Her father swore, rushing at Joanna.

She held the keys behind her, so terrified she couldn't move.

"Give them to me!" he snarled. "Give me those keys!"

Could this be her father? she thought, appalled. He looked like a wild animal. She hated him, hated him!

He grabbed her roughly, tore the keys from her hands, and cursed. "Give me those keys! I'm getting out of here!"

"Look at you!" their mother screamed after him. "Drunk in front of your children!"

It's my fault that he has the keys, Joanna thought. "Daddy, please don't drive—"

"Shut up!" he snapped, rushing out. He flung the

words behind him. "You have to drag your little sister to those hypocrites, too?"

A terrible silence filled the room as the three of them heard the car start up, then leave.

"I'm sorry, Mom," Joanna said. "I'm sorry about the keys. I couldn't help it." She wished her mother would cry, she looked so miserable. Did she hate Dad too when he was like this?

Her mother found a tissue and blotted the blood on her lip. "I'm sorry you girls had to see this. He needs help. He can't stop drinking by himself anymore."

Joanna recalled commercials on television about clinics for alcoholics. "Everyone will find out."

Her mother looked resigned. "People are going to find out even more if he kills someone with the car," Mom said.

Cathy sobbed. "He isn't like Daddy anymore."

Her mother hugged her. "He's not himself. He's really not himself when he drinks."

But who is he? Joanna wondered.

Her mother gave Cathy a squeeze. "Why don't you girls go to a movie or something this afternoon to get your minds off of this mess?"

She was right, Joanna thought. They had to get out. Especially Cathy. "Maybe we could go horseback riding at Heidi's. She's always inviting me."

"Sounds like a good idea," her mother answered. "What do you think, Cathy?"

Cathy nodded, her usual enthusiasm gone.

Joanna started for the phone. "I'll call Heidi now."

———

That afternoon on the dusty riding trail Heidi led the way astride her black mare. Next came Cathy, her pigtails bobbing up and down as she bounced along on

Heidi's old pony, Dolly. Joanna rode a big chestnut horse, feeling better as they made their way through slanting shafts of sunshine among the eucalyptus trees. Was Cathy forgetting what had happened at home after church? she wondered. Probably not. Probably never. She hoped Cathy wouldn't begin to hate their father, too.

The soft clip-clop of the horses' hooves and the trill of birds filled the sunny afternoon. The smell of horses hung pleasantly in the autumn air. As the trail widened, Heidi reined in her horse, waiting for Cathy and Joanna. "I don't know who's enjoying this more, you or Dolly," she said to Cathy.

"Me, I think," Cathy said, rubbing Dolly's neck and managing a smile.

Joanna felt more and more secure with the warmth and sure strength of the big chestnut under her. It felt as if he were taking care of her, soothing her as they moved along the trail.

Again, rays of sunshine slanted through the eucalyptus trees, and suddenly she remembered her grandfather calling the sun's rays the fingers of God.

"You could come riding with me most Sundays," Heidi said as the three of them rode side by side. "Sometimes I'm lonely without sisters or brothers."

Even without sisters or brothers, Heidi seemed happy most of the time, Joanna thought. Heidi's parents, elderly and European, were different from most American parents, but they seemed kind and loving.

"Do you go to church on Sundays?" Joanna asked without thinking.

Heidi gave a laugh. "No. Should I?"

Joanna felt her face getting red. "I don't know." She patted her horse's soft, warm neck. "I usually don't either, but we went with David Porter this morning."

"In my family," Heidi said with a rueful smile, "work is our god—medicine for my father, the chemistry lab for my mother. I don't know what they'd do if they had to give up working. It really is their lives."

In a way work was already Heidi's life, too, Joanna thought. Veterinary school was all that Heidi seemed to think about. "Did your father ever think about being a vet?" she asked.

"He says he still does when people are unpleasant," Heidi said. "Horses are usually nicer than people."

Maybe it was better to have horses as friends, Joanna decided. Heidi seemed happier than most people who had humans for friends. But was Heidi facing reality?

Later Heidi's parents insisted that Joanna and Cathy stay for a simple supper of homemade soup and sandwiches. Despite her parents' Austrian accents and their different ways, Joanna didn't know when she had had a nicer Sunday afternoon in a long time.

As Joanna and Cathy drove home, they talked about Heidi and her family. "You know," Joanna said, "we can be different, too. Maybe if we just try hard enough, we can change things at home."

"Let's do it," Cathy answered. "Let's really try."

When they walked into the house, their mother was waiting uneasily. "We have to be quiet," she told them. "There's a man from Dad's office in the den talking to him about AA—you know, Alcoholics Anonymous."

"How did that happen?" Joanna asked.

"He saw Dad out drinking on the beach. He talked him into coming home."

Cathy's face turned pale. "You mean Dad is an . . . an alcoholic?"

"Yes," their mother said firmly. "Yes, he's an alcoholic, and we have to face it."

Cathy turned to Joanna. "Do you think we can change that?"

Joanna shook her head. She felt like crying, even more for Cathy and her mother than for herself. Most of all for her father. He looked so miserably unhappy when he was drunk.

"Maybe we should pray," Cathy said, tears rolling down her cheeks.

It certainly hadn't done any good so far, Joanna thought, but why not let Cathy have some hope? "Good idea," she said. What could Cathy's praying hurt anyhow?

10

$\mathcal{G}$lancing out the kitchen windows on Thanksgiving afternoon, Joanna was pleased it was such a sunny day. She swirled whipped cream on top of the pumpkin pies. Despite her problems, she did have a lot to be thankful for. For one thing, she and Matt had dated steadily for almost a month now, and although he had yet to say he loved her, he would. Someday he'd get over loving Melanie.

She glanced at her mother, who leaned over the oven basting the slowly browning turkey. She seemed more nervous lately; she was always taking tranquilizers. She'd popped two a while ago.

Cutting carrot and celery sticks by the kitchen sink, Cathy was singing a Thanksgiving song she'd learned at school. She seemed happier today than she'd been for a while. Outside, their father swept the sidewalk and blacktop driveway in preparation for their guests. He was not drinking nowadays. His AA friend picked him up for meetings three or four nights a week.

Just three weeks ago her family had seemed to be coming apart. Who could have dreamed that they would be having Thanksgiving dinner at their house? Even Matt was coming, and so were David and his parents, and Dede with hers.

Cathy looked up from over the sink. "Dede could hardly believe we'd invite their family. They were going

117

to have a plain old dinner, just the three of them."

"Maybe we should do things like this more often," Joanna said. The smell of roasting turkey made the day feel the way Thanksgiving should, and it had been fun to get everything ready for the guests. This morning they'd decorated the front door with an Indian corn arrangement. In the dining room they used a gold tablecloth and orange napkins on the table. In its center they placed a rattan cornucopia overflowing with apples, pears, nuts, and bananas. It looked perfect.

Her mother pushed the basted turkey back into the oven. "I hope this dinner works out. After all, we hardly know any of our guests well."

"It'll be fine, Mom. And if they don't like apple juice or milk, that's just too bad."

Her mother glanced at her sharply. "I don't know. I feel as if it's the calm before the storm."

Why couldn't her mother be happy now that things were going well? Joanna wondered. Mom had become so negative.

Their guests were to arrive at three o'clock, but the doorbell rang at two-thirty. Joanna ran for the door, still in her old ragged jeans.

Matt stood there, grinning sheepishly, his hand holding something behind him. "I'm early."

She smiled. "You sure are. I'm going to put you to work."

He held out a big box of chocolates like a peace offering, and she couldn't help laughing. "It's for your mother."

She reached up to kiss his cheek. "You get out of working after all."

"I'd just as soon help. It's so quiet at home alone." He smiled. "Wow, it sure smells good."

She was so glad Mom had let her invite him. He was

lonely with his dad out of town and Rena in Los Angeles with her family. "I should have told you to be here to help at seven this morning," she said teasingly.

"I'd have been here . . . well, maybe."

"You can help Dad watch the football game," she said, taking him into the family room.

He and her father shook hands and made small talk before settling down to watch the game. There was a comfortable feeling in the room, she thought as she hurried to her bedroom.

After a fast shower, she slipped into a green tank dress and matching blouse.

When Joanna stepped out of her bedroom, the other guests were arriving at the front door. Dede was already admiring Cathy's new outfit and everyone was shaking hands, looking pleased about Thanksgiving. Her mother accepted a pot of yellow chrysanthemums from David's mother.

Then Joanna saw them—gift-wrapped bottles the men handed to her father.

"White wine to go with the turkey," Dede's father said.

David's father chuckled. "Same here. Not too original."

Her father thanked them, smiling.

What if he can't handle this? she thought, not knowing what to do. She couldn't just grab the wine bottles from her father's hands.

"Shall we refrigerate the wine until dinner?" her mother asked. "Perhaps Joanna can take them."

Her father handed the bottles to her, avoiding her eyes.

The difficult moment was over, she thought as she hurried to the kitchen with the wine. But now they would have to offer the wine at dinner.

When she returned to the living room with raw vegetables and dips, everything seemed fine.

Later, as they walked into the dining room, their guests admired the turkey and festive decorations.

Joanna and Matt served apple juice, milk, and wine as her father carved the turkey. She worried that his hand might shake the way it did sometimes lately, but everything went well. When she came to his goblet, she simply filled it with apple juice. Only David's and Dede's parents were drinking wine anyhow. Even Matt had decided on apple juice, probably to impress her parents.

There was a moment of silence as everyone was finally served. "David," her mother said into the quiet, "would you like to say a prayer? David's grandfather was a minister, you know," she explained to Dede's parents.

David nodded and bowed his head. "Heavenly Father," he said, "we come before you today full of thanksgiving for our friendships, for your love . . ."

He went on, but fortunately the prayer was short. Prayers seemed strange in their house anyhow, although Cathy went to Sunday school now with Dede.

Joanna glanced at Matt. Maybe he would think they were religious nuts.

He smiled at her happily, as if he hadn't given the idea a thought and as if he were having a wonderful time. If only he would love her someday as much as she loved him. Nothing would make her more thankful.

11

"Aren't we going to decorate for Christmas?" Rena asked Matt and Joanna the Saturday before school was out. They were sitting at the kitchen counter at his house, eating chips and one of Rena's health food dips. "It's so much fun to put up a tree," Rena added, hopeful.

Joanna smiled. Rena was always so enthusiastic about everything that sometimes she seemed younger than Joanna and Matt, and she had to be at least fifty.

Matt shrugged. "I don't feel much like decorating. No one's going to be around except us anyhow."

Joanna wished he would do something, anything. He was becoming more and more depressed all the time. She thought he would be over Melanie by now, but he was forever talking about her, blaming himself.

Basketball season was getting him down, too. Despite having been captain of last year's team, he refused even to go to games now. Instead, he took his back pain pills.

"The realtors said that Christmas decorations are good for showing the house," Rena said. "We could at least have a tree."

"Okay, okay." Matt looked angry. "But not one of those gold ribbony ones like Dad's decorator girlfriend talked us into last year."

Joanna and Rena exchanged a glance.

"Anyhow," he continued, "Mom took all the Christmas ornaments. All we have are those gold balls from last year."

"Sounds like a department store tree," Joanna ventured.

"I've seen better in stores," Matt answered.

Joanna thought about her family's usual Christmas trees and the faded ornaments that went all the way back to her grandparents' lives. Mom had insisted that the ornaments be moved with them to California, no matter how much it might cost. Decorating the tree was always one of the happiest times of the year for her family.

"How about if we string popcorn and cranberries?" Rena suggested. "We could even make dough ornaments."

Matt's eyes lit up. "I guess we could."

"You two go buy the tree, and I'll shop for everything else," Rena said.

"Would your father mind?" Joanna asked, although she really wondered whether they could afford it. Matt's father had sold a lot of his stocks and bonds. After the first week there hadn't been many prospective buyers for their house, and the sailboat hadn't sold yet either.

"Why should he mind?" Matt snapped. "He's not even going to be here for Christmas. He's going skiing in Utah."

Joanna wondered how his father could afford that when Matt was concerned about having enough money for college.

"Why don't we decide to have a wonderful Christmas?" Rena suggested. "You know, just make that decision, and then do it."

"Okay," Matt answered flatly. "I decide to have a wonderful Christmas."

"Come on, Matt," Joanna said, trying to cheer him. "I second the motion. We're going to have a wonderful Christmas!"

Matt got up. "So I'll run upstairs and get into my old jeans. Then we'll buy a tree."

Rena waited until he left, then sat down on the stool next to Joanna. "I'm concerned about him," she said.

"Me too."

"I wonder," Rena began, thoughtful, "do you suppose he'd attend church with you?"

"With me? But I don't even go."

Rena raised an eyebrow. "I felt sure you did."

"Why would you ever think that?" Joanna asked.

"Your eyes," Rena said. "Haven't you ever heard that saying, 'The eyes are the windows of the soul'? You can see quite a lot in people's eyes."

Joanna backed away on her stool, not liking the drift of their conversation. "What do you see in my eyes?"

"A softness, a vulnerability that you don't hide nearly as well as you think."

How could she see that? Joanna wondered, although she had a feeling about eyes, too. Some people wouldn't look you in the eye for anything, and others stared you down with hard, steely eyes. Most didn't really let you look too deeply into their eyes, as if they might be too revealing.

She remembered Melanie's beautiful violet eyes. Anger. They held glints of anger.

Rena smiled, and it occurred to Joanna that Rena's eyes usually held enthusiasm and . . . wonder.

"I recognized your troubled spirit, Joanna, the first day I met you. It's as if God told me to tell you how much He loves you. He wants you to put your life in His hands."

Joanna backed away, getting off her barstool. "How would you know?"

"Because God desires for everyone to be a child of His."

Joanna looked away quickly. "If I'm His child, why do so many bad things happen around me? Look at Melanie . . . and now Matt. And there are others." Her father came to mind.

"Evil exists, too," Rena said. "There are bad spirits in the world . . . spirits of anger, suicide, lust, drunkenness, divisiveness."

Maybe she's crazy, Joanna thought. She wanted to get away from the conversation, to run from the room, but she recalled her grandfather telling her about Jesus. "My grandfather was a Christian," she found herself saying as she sat down on the next barstool to put more space between them. "I was just a little girl, but I remember sitting with him looking at a sunset. He told me how much God loves us."

She looked at Rena. "When he talked about God, his eyes were bright, so full of light . . . like yours." She suddenly felt embarrassed. "Anyway, if there's a heaven, my grandfather must be there."

Matt came around the corner. "Hey, I don't need to hear any talk about dying! Come on, let's get the tree."

Joanna wondered how much he'd heard.

She could feel Rena watching her as they left. Probably Rena was praying for her and Matt, even with her eyes open.

It turned out to be a good day, Joanna thought that evening as Matt drove her home. He'd finally overcome his depression as they decorated the Christmas tree, and they'd laughed crazily with Rena. He had almost been the old Matt, and they had felt almost like a family.

When they drove up the road to her house, all the

outside lights were on—and a police car stood in the driveway!

"What could be wrong?" Joanna gasped as they rushed from Matt's car. Then it began to dawn on her. Dad . . . something about Dad!

An ambulance siren wailed up the road, and she and Matt raced to the house.

She threw the door open, then stopped. Cathy's face and her mother's face were bruised and beaten, their clothing torn. Joanna screamed until Matt grabbed her and shook her.

She turned to the wild man being subdued by the police in the family room. Her father!

"Lemme alone!" he shouted at the two policemen. "It's my house, my house!"

"Dad!" Joanna cried in horror.

As he turned to her, the policemen got a firm hold on him. "You brought 'em! You brought these cops!" His eyes were so angry that they frightened her more than his words.

"I promise I didn't!"

He didn't seem to hear. "I'll blacken your eyes—blacken your eyes! Boyfriend's too!"

She hated him! She'd never hated anyone so much in her life!

"He's going to a hospital," her mother said, her voice shaking. "I can't take it anymore. I just can't take it! They know how to deal with alcoholics there."

"When did he start drinking again?" Joanna asked.

"I don't know," her mother answered. "There was nothing I could do."

Matt turned to Joanna. "Guess I'd better go."

She scarcely heard him.

Ambulance attendants rushed in, and before she knew what had happened, her father was gone. When it was all over and the police were leaving, she looked for Matt.

Gone too. . . !

She knew that nothing, absolutely nothing would ever be the same between her and Matt again.

12

At Santa Rosita High, Matt avoided Joanna between classes, and when they happened to pass each other, he pretended not to see her. Everyone knew that Joanna Stevens was not Matt Thompson's girl anymore.

During the first tearful days she thought that he didn't want anything to do with a girl whose father was a drunk. Then she remembered how he'd tried to help Melanie, how his parents' divorce must have hurt him, how his back injury had ruined basketball for him. And now there were his father's money problems, too. She finally decided that Matt just couldn't face any more trouble—that was why he'd run out on her.

Someone said that he was taking Josie Jensen to a Christmas party, and Joanna thought she might die. How could he? Everyone knew Josie's bad reputation.

Over Christmas vacation Joanna began to buy bottles of wine and sherry when she did the family grocery shopping for her mother. The check-out clerks, busy with long lines of Christmas shoppers, didn't even ask for an ID.

By the middle of January she was rushing home after school for a glass or two of wine, unable to stop drinking. The check-out clerks still didn't question her as she bought more wine, even though the Christmas crush of customers had ended.

The wine in her closet and under her bathroom sink disappeared so quickly that she couldn't believe she was drinking it all, and she'd already taken as much of the wine and liqueurs from the kitchen cabinet as she dared.

Crying in bed at night, she would relive the wonderful moments with Matt. What was the sense in living without him?

In February, on Washington's Birthday, Matt called. At first she thought it was a dream, but it was Matt. It really was him.

"Joanna?" he repeated as she stood speechless at the phone. "I've missed you so much." His voice quavered. "Can we go somewhere tonight?"

She stared at the phone. She mustn't sound too eager. From the way he avoided her at school she'd been sure that everything was over between them, yet she'd never stopped loving him.

"Sure, Matt," she said, trying to sound calm. "Tonight is fine." She hadn't had a date with anyone during those terrible nine weeks, even though David had asked her to one of his church parties.

"How about a movie?" Matt asked.

"That's . . . that's fine."

"I'll pick you up at seven," he said. "Bye, Joanna."

"Bye, Matt," she managed to say without sounding too thrilled. *He'd missed her! He'd missed her just as she'd missed him!*

"It was Matt!" she told her mother and Cathy. "He asked me out for tonight!" She whirled around with happiness.

Her mother smiled. "I thought that he might sometime again."

"I prayed about it for you," Cathy said.

"You prayed?"

Cathy nodded. "At Sunday school our teacher says that prayer is the biggest power on earth. She says that God hears every prayer."

Joanna caught her mother's eye. She shrugged as if to say, "She's little, humor her."

"I prayed for Dad, too," Cathy added. "Then he came home from the hospital right after."

"That's nice, honey," her mother said and started for the kitchen. "We'll eat early since you have a date, Joanna."

Cathy looked disappointed. "Mom doesn't believe me, but Dad did come home early—for Christmas, just like I prayed."

Joanna recalled Cathy's excitement when their father was allowed to come home early. It was as if she'd expected a miracle and got it.

Well, their father had given up drinking. Yet something had gone out of him. He seemed sad and empty— even at Christmas. Either he brought home papers from his office and worked in the den evenings, or he watched TV. There was nothing happy about his life now, just when it seemed there should be.

Joanna patted Cathy's shoulder. "I think it's more that Mom would rather forget Dad being in the hospital. It's better not to dwell on bad times."

"I prayed for you and for Matt, too," Cathy said. "I asked God to touch your hearts."

Now where had she heard that? Maybe Cathy shouldn't go to that Sunday school or she could turn into one of those religious types, too. "Thanks, Cathy. I have to go wash my hair now."

Joanna hurried to her room, nearly floating as she thought about Matt. What should she wear? What should she do with her hair? In her bathroom she was suddenly overcome with tears. She was going out with

Matt again! He had missed her! She sat down on the bathroom floor, both laughing and crying. She'd have to be careful what she said to him. Maybe they could start all over. Her hands shook. Opening the bathroom sink cabinet, she reached for the sherry. There was very little left.

After dinner she slipped into her new sweater and jeans, then glanced into the mirror. Her eyes were bloodshot. Well, eye drops would fix that. Eye drops, mouthwash, aspirin, antacid tablets. It had become a twice-a-day routine.

That evening, when she opened the front door, Matt smiled uneasily. "How are you, Joanna?" he asked.

She felt like a stranger. "Fine," she answered, looking into his eyes. They stood staring at each other, smiling shyly.

As they walked out to the car, she was surprised to see an old brown two-door Chevrolet.

"We sold the Corvette," he said, holding the door open for her. He sounded resigned.

She didn't know what to say. "This car looks all right."

"Yeah. It's okay."

As Matt walked around the back of the car, Joanna felt as if this were their first date.

He slid into his seat, slammed the door, and turned to her.

"Oh, Matt," she said, "the car doesn't matter! I've missed you so much."

She was in his arms, tears rolling down her cheeks, remembering again how wonderful it felt just to have him hold her. Maybe she was throwing herself at him, but it didn't matter. Nothing mattered if she could only stay in his arms.

"I love you," he said. "I love you, Joanna."

He *did* love her! He did! She thought that her heart might burst with happiness. If it took weeks of agony to make him realize he loved her it was worth it.

In the dim light they gazed at each other, then their lips met. His arms tightened around her until she thought she might be crushed.

When they moved away to catch their breath, his elbow touched the horn. It blasted out into the night for a second. They glanced at each other in panic, then began to laugh.

"We'd better go." He started the car. "Do you still want to go to a movie?"

"No," she said, "but maybe we should, Matt."

He nodded, then smiled at her. "Yeah, we'd better."

The movie was a spy thriller, but Joanna could scarcely follow the plot as she sat with Matt's arm around her, his other hand holding hers. She felt encircled with his love. He kissed her forehead, her cheek, her hand. She never wanted to be away from him again.

As they left the theater, Matt stopped at the drinking fountain in the lobby and popped a pill into his mouth.

Joanna felt a stab of terror. He was still taking those drugs!

His hand slipped into hers as they walked out the theater door.

"Is your back still bothering you?" she asked.

"Yeah." He squeezed her hand.

"It's just that I'm worried you might get hooked on those pills. You know the movies about drugs they're always showing at school."

"No nagging," he shot back.

She decided to drop the subject. Anyhow, his pills were prescribed by a doctor. She reached up to kiss his cheek. "Sorry. I promise, no nagging."

He looked down at her tenderly. "You'd better not."

She knew it was an order.

"You want to go to Morelli's for pizza?" he asked.

"Sounds great," she said. They'd have fun tonight, no matter what.

They headed across the parking lot for Morelli's blinking Christmas lights that were left up all year. The red PIZZA sign glowed through the night across the far end of the shopping center.

She wondered if anyone from school would be there. Probably. Morelli's pizza, spaghetti, and lasagna, the best in town, attracted everyone—high school kids, college kids, families.

She and Matt stepped into Morelli's dimly lit entry. The place was crowded as usual.

As they waited for the hostess, Chad stood up at a distant table and waved them over. There were eight kids from school at the long table but room for two more.

"You want to sit with them?" Matt asked.

She wasn't certain, but Matt looked as if he wanted to. "Why not?"

She'd rather have him to herself, she thought as she started for Chad's table, but the popular crowd had hardly noticed her since she and Matt quit dating.

"Hi!" The timing couldn't be better for them to see her and Matt together.

Curiosity danced in everyone's eyes as Matt seated her. She smiled up at him. "Thank you, sir."

Their eyes held for a wondrous moment so full of love that she knew anyone watching would know Matt loved her.

As Matt sat down, Chad poked her with his elbow and whispered, "I didn't think anyone would ever make old Matt look like that again."

She smiled, despite Chad's word *again*, which reminded her that Matt had once gazed like that at Melanie.

Matt slid his arm around Joanna's shoulder and gave her a squeeze. Was he jealous of Chad's whispering to her? She hoped so.

She turned to Matt and, from the look in his eyes, thought he might kiss her, right in front of everyone. Then he backed off, aware that the waitress was hovering over them for their order. His lingering smile touched her heart. She'd never had anyone love her so much that he let everyone else around know it, too.

At the table, the girls looked jealous; the boys, curious.

Chad's date, Sue Martin, was last year's prom queen. Josie Jensen, whom Matt had taken out over Christmas vacation, was there with Tad Johnson, football team captain. Two of the girls, Teri and Sally, were cheerleaders and their dates, Tom Hogan and Ron Saager, were stars of the basketball team.

If she'd chosen who might see her with Matt tonight, she couldn't have done better. These were just the right people to see them together.

Matt put his arm around her again, and she nearly melted as he held her hair away from her ear and whispered, "You're the most beautiful girl here."

"You're crazy."

He shook his head, and she could see that he meant it. He really meant she was the most beautiful girl here. Maybe it was true that love blinded people. She glanced at Josie, Sue, Teri, and Sally. She wasn't as pretty as any of them, but Matt thought so. She wondered if he thought she was more beautiful than Melanie had been.

As they sat there, eating pizza and laughing, Joanna couldn't help looking at Matt over and over to be sure this wasn't a dream.

Ron Saager interrupted her thoughts, "We're having a big keg blast at my house tomorrow night. Can you two make it?"

Matt glanced at Joanna, and she nodded. It seemed as if they didn't even need words anymore. "Sure," Matt said, his eyes still on her.

Later, after they had eaten and the group was breaking up, Matt whispered, "Let's go to my house. No one will be home."

Fear flickered through her, but as his arm tightened around her waist, she didn't care what happened. She only wanted to be in his arms. "Okay."

In the dimly lit parking lot they stopped by the car door. He leaned down and kissed her tenderly, then again with a sweet longing.

"Hey, what is this?" Tad Johnson laughed as he and Josie passed by, going to their car.

"This scene is better than the movies," someone else joked.

"Never mind," Matt told them.

"They're just jealous," he whispered to her. Then his lips touched hers again.

For a moment she wondered what Josie Jensen thought, then forgot about her, Tad, and everyone else.

Matt finally moved away. "Wow! Let's go!"

In the car she sat close to him, his arm around her. "At least it's better than a car with bucket seats," she said, thinking about the red Corvette.

"The only good difference," he answered, leaning down to kiss her hair.

As they drove up Matt's street, she wondered if his father or Rena might come home unexpectedly, but the house was dark except for the lights by the front door.

Inside, Matt headed for the den. "Let's have a drink and watch TV."

"Great!" She needed a drink. She glanced with him into the bar refrigerator.

"Looks like Dad left a whole pitcher of margaritas. You want to try some?"

She wasn't sure. She didn't want to drink hard liquor. "Is it strong?"

He laughed. "Like lemonade."

"Okay, why not?"

She helped him carry glasses, peanuts, and napkins to the coffee table in front of the brown leather couch.

He put the frosty pitcher on the table in front of them and turned on the TV. "What do you want to watch?"

"It doesn't matter," she said. All she wanted was to be with him. She poured the margaritas into their glasses and tasted hers. It was good. Taking a long drink, she felt the familiar warm glow spreading through her. She filled her glass to the top again, smiling at Matt as he came to her.

"I love you, Joanna," he said.

She opened her arms to him.

It was two o'clock when they realized how late it was. They had drunk the whole pitcher of margaritas.

Joanna giggled as she tried to stand up. "Do you think we drank too much?"

Matt got up and was tottering, too. "And we're going to a party tomorrow night!"

They dissolved into laughter.

"You know, you're even more beautiful when you laugh," he said, leaning down for another kiss.

She ducked away and ran for the front door. "I've got to get home. Mom will have a fit."

He chased her to the car, laughing, and she didn't know when she had ever been so happy. Everything was perfect.

13

$\mathcal{D}$espite a hangover, Joanna rushed through her Saturday house cleaning chores in the morning so she could spend the afternoon with Matt at the Santa Rosita Library. She had a term paper due in U.S. history. His paper was in American government.

The phone rang at one o'clock.

"Telephone, Joanna!" Cathy called out. She grinned as she gave the phone to Joanna in the hallway. "It's Matt," she whispered, her hand carefully over the mouthpiece.

Strange, Joanna thought, taking the phone. Matt was due right now. "You're going to be late," she guessed.

"I can't take you to the library after all," he said. "Dad thinks we have a buyer for the sailboat. He wants me to help him show it in half an hour."

During the nine weeks they had been apart, she hadn't thought much about the sailboat being for sale or whether it'd been sold. "I'll miss you, Matt."

At least they would be going to Ron Saager's keg party together tonight, she thought when she drove to the library alone. If Matt's father did sell the sailboat today, she hoped it wouldn't put Matt in a bad mood for the party.

After dinner she changed into her new jeans and a soft angora sweater, hoping it was the right outfit to wear to a keg party.

Just when she was ready, Cathy knocked on the bedroom door. "Matt's here! Dad's talking to him."

Joanna rushed down the hallway to the family room and saw with relief that Matt and her father were having a pleasant conversation. Lately her father had been more agreeable, as if he were trying to make amends for the horrible times he'd put them through. Still, she couldn't forgive him.

Her mother was just stepping into the family room, too.

"Hi," Joanna said as Matt's eyes turned to her.

His face lit up. "Hi."

In the silence her whole family looked at them as if they knew she and Matt loved each other.

Later, as they walked to the car in the darkness, Matt asked, "Do you think everyone can see we're in love?"

She smiled. "I hope so."

Matt laughed, turning to her for a kiss. It was then that she first noticed the smell of alcohol on his breath.

"You sold the sailboat," she guessed as they climbed into his old brown Chevrolet.

"Yeah. How did you know?" he asked.

Because you've been drinking, she thought, but she said, "I just had a feeling you'd sell it today."

"Let's not talk about it," he said as he drove down the road.

He'd taken her out sailing two magnificent Sundays last fall. She remembered seeing him on the dock with the sailboat, the breeze blowing his hair, the sun shining on him as if nothing would ever change.

She moved closer to him, and he squeezed her hand.

As they pulled out onto the main road, she recalled the first time he'd picked her up at the school bus stop. How much fun he'd been before Melanie's suicide and his father's money problems.

"Where does Ron Saager live?" she asked.

"Santa Rosita Hills."

She darted a glance at him, wondering if driving there reminded him of his old house or of Melanie. There seemed no way of getting Matt away from his problems.

She was grateful, at least, that basketball season was finally over. Ron was star of the basketball team now that Matt couldn't play. The team hadn't made it to the play-offs this year without him. Would most of the team be at the party? She hoped not. They'd only be another sad reminder for Matt.

As they pulled into Ron's driveway, Joanna was surprised to see an unpretentious brown shake house. She brushed her hair hurriedly as they drove around back where the other cars were parked. "Looks like a big party."

Music throbbed into the darkness from the building behind the house. "It's their old stables," Matt explained. "When they sold their horses they converted the stables into a guesthouse and party rooms. It's a great place."

Joanna was glad she'd worn jeans, since everyone else getting out of cars looked very casual.

As she and Matt walked into the converted stables, the party was going full blast. A few kids were dancing to the wild beat of the music, but most of them congregated around the keg, glass beer mugs in hand. The sweet smell of marijuana hung in the air.

"Hey, Matt! Joanna!" Ron called out, and soon everyone was greeting them.

Joanna could feel people looking at her, some surprised she and Matt were together again. Others must have heard from the group at Morelli's last night.

Matt handed her a frosty mug of beer. "It's all they have to drink."

She hadn't really liked beer when she'd tried it at Matt's one afternoon, but decided she'd learn to like it. She smiled up at Matt and took a sip. "It's good," she said. It was, maybe because it was keg beer and she was so thirsty.

"Hi, Joanna." It was Sue Martin smiling at her.

"Hi, Sue."

Nearby, Josie Jensen, her black sweater and jeans far too tight, smiled up at Matt as if Joanna didn't exist. Josie's blond hair fell in soft waves to the shoulders of her black sweater. Her big blue eyes swam with secrets as she looked at Matt.

Joanna felt a surge of anger. First it had been Melanie, now girls like Josie after Matt. Joanna gulped her beer.

Matt smiled as if he knew she was jealous. "You want another beer?"

"Not yet." Her mug was still more than half full, and she was surprised to see Matt had already downed his.

He started for the keg. "I'm getting another."

She saw Josie turn to follow him, her hand reaching for his arm.

"Matt! Just a minute." Joanna gulped her beer as she hurried behind him. "I'm coming."

Josie stopped to talk to someone else, but her cheeks dimpled with amusement as Joanna passed.

Josie would make a play for Matt as soon as she grew tired of Tad Johnson, Joanna thought. Josie collected boyfriends as if they were blue ribbons.

Matt waited until Joanna caught up.

She suddenly wished that Matt would hold her hand, but he was too busy talking to everyone around them. Tonight it took an effort to look as if she were having a good time.

As he filled their mugs, Chad winked at her.

Joanna smiled, wondering if he'd seen the episode with Josie. Chad never seemed to miss much.

Matt must have noticed something odd because his attention shifted to her, maybe because of Chad or maybe because everyone was talking about the final basketball game. It had been a wild overtime, the game of the season, but Santa Rosita High had lost.

Matt led her to the long wooden bench lining the back wall of the room. "Still love me?" he whispered as they sat down. He slipped an arm around her shoulders.

"Usually," she answered with irritation, then was surprised her annoyance with him and Josie had surfaced so clearly.

He was taken aback, too. After a moment, he said, "Joanna, I want you to stay away from Chad. I heard about him chasing you at Melanie's party. I know he's been watching you."

Well, what about you and Josie? she thought.

"You're my girl," he whispered, tightening his arm around her shoulder.

She smiled and sipped her beer. If Chad was so interested in her, why hadn't he called for a date when she and Matt weren't dating? All that time Chad had kept a cautious distance.

She looked up at Matt, glad to see him jealous.

"What's wrong?" he asked.

"Nothing now." Her love must have shown in her eyes, though, because suddenly his lips were on hers. Oh, she did love him so! Yet it seemed as if one of them always had to love more than the other did, and right now, she felt as if she were the one who loved most. She pushed him away gently. "Not here in front of everyone."

"Later?" he asked. She nodded, smiling. Maybe that way they'd leave early, getting away from girls like Josie.

Strange. She'd never thought he'd be interested in a girl with Josie's reputation, maybe because Melanie had gotten herself into such trouble.

He got up with a grin, pulling her up, too. "Well, if we're not going to kiss, let's drink."

Joanna laughed.

The rest of the evening he stayed close to her, occasionally glancing at Chad. There would be no question in anyone's mind: Matt Thompson was hers.

During the next month there were keg parties every weekend at different houses. None of the parents were ever around, but why worry her family about that? Joanna thought. Anyhow, her mother was too busy with working now, and her father had turned inward, as if he didn't care. Cathy was the only one really interested in Matt and the parties.

"I'm going to have to have a party at my house before it's sold," Matt said one day at school. "Maybe the first weekend in April. The weather will be better, and we can have it out on the patio by the ocean."

"What about your father?" she asked.

"He'll be in Hawaii on business."

"Wouldn't Rena have a fit?"

Matt shrugged. "I don't think she'll be there. I heard her on the phone—" Someone interrupted, and Matt never finished whatever he meant to say.

———

The next day after school Matt was upstairs getting a book from his room when Joanna saw Rena.

"I'm afraid I'm moving to Los Angeles," Rena told her. "Since the house is for sale, I've had to keep my eyes open for a job."

Joanna knew that Rena needed to work, since she was a widow with little money. Still, she acted as if life were an adventure.

"The realtors say the house will probably sell soon," Rena said. "I know Matt and his father will find a beautiful condo to live in. They won't need me to run things anymore."

"I don't know how he'll take moving into a little condo."

Rena's eyes filled with light. "Will you hold my hands and pray for Matt?"

"No, thanks. I'd rather not," Joanna answered stiffly. She escaped to Matt in the kitchen as Rena closed her eyes in prayer. Thank goodness she was leaving!

Rena was gone by the first of April.

"At least the house is clean," Joanna said the Saturday afternoon of Matt's keg party. They still had a cleaning woman once a week so the house would be presentable for prospective buyers. "All we have to do is get glasses."

"No. The Keg Place furnishes the beer mugs, too," Matt explained. He'd phoned The Keg Place and ordered beer two weeks ago simply by charging it to his father's credit card. They'd deliver the kegs and the mugs anytime now. Matt's father's accountant would never even ask about the bill.

"Do you want me to buy pretzels and chips?" Joanna asked.

"Great. I'll hang around for the keg delivery."

It made her feel a bit shy, helping with arrangements for a party at his house. If Matt had a mother around, she probably wouldn't want a girlfriend playing hostess.

Or maybe he wouldn't be having a drinking party at all.

The kitchen phone rang, and Joanna looked to see if Matt was going to answer it. Instead, he was sneaking a pill at the kitchen sink. Well, it wasn't worth an argument. She picked up the phone. "Thompson residence."

After a slight pause, a girl asked for Matt. Joanna was sure it was Josie Jensen. Of all the nerve! she thought, handing the phone to Matt and turning away.

"Sure," he was saying. "Come anyhow. Don't worry about it."

When he hung up, he said, "Tad can't come. Josie wondered if she could come without a date."

"Oh," Joanna said. "Well, great." She grabbed Matt's car keys from the kitchen counter. "I'll get the pretzels and chips."

In the car she decided to forget about Josie. It was too beautiful a day to be upset, especially here where she could see the ocean from every street corner. Bursts of bougainvillea bloomed against walls and fences, and flowering trees blossomed pink and white from the March rains.

Joanna wondered how Matt would feel if he did move to a small condo. He never talked about it. In fact, he'd never even mentioned the sailboat after it was sold, and he never mentioned Melanie either. Maybe that was why he drank so much now.

By seven o'clock she and Matt had moved the outdoor furniture to the back patio, and the keg of beer and mugs were set up on the redwood table. As Matt put down his end of a redwood bench, he grimaced with pain.

"You'd better take a pill for your back, Matt," she found herself saying.

"I already took more than I'm supposed to."

"Oh, Matt!" She thought he had been taking far too many of the pain pills for the last few weeks, and both of them had been drinking more than usual, too. She started to say more but saw a flicker of warning in his green eyes. "Okay. I won't nag."

He grinned. "Thanks."

They'd stuck two signs on the house. Each said PARTY, and arrows on them directed everyone around back. As people began to arrive, Joanna rushed in to put on lipstick and give her hair a fast brushing.

Glancing in the guest bathroom mirror, she wondered if Matt still thought her beautiful. He didn't say so anymore unless she asked him.

She started back out to the party, then stopped at the den's sliding glass door.

Josie was arriving, her blond hair shining against the sunset. Her tight blue T-shirt matched her blue eyes, and she wore the shortest mini-skirt Joanna had ever seen.

Matt's back was to Josie, and she tiptoed to him. Smiling, she caught him in a big hug.

Joanna could see Matt's eyes suddenly open wide as Josie pressed against him. Then he was laughing with everyone else as Josie slipped her arm around his waist as if they were just old buddies. Josie took a long drink from Matt's beer mug, then smiled up at him, her blue eyes soft with secrets.

14

*J*oanna felt as if everyone were watching her as she opened the sliding glass door and stepped out into the glow of the sunset. The orange and golden radiance hung over the patio, reflecting off the doors and the glass panels in the fence until they were suffused with color and light.

Through the glow she saw Josie still had an arm around Matt's waist, and he had an arm casually draped over her shoulders. He didn't even look embarrassed! Joanna fumed. In fact, he seemed to think there was nothing wrong about it. He was enjoying every moment of holding Josie!

Joanna headed for the beer keg, trying to hide her anger.

"Looks like you need a beer," Chad remarked.

She hadn't even noticed him standing by the keg. He was right, though. She tried to concentrate on the foam rising in the glass mug as Chad filled it for her. Actually, she'd like to have two beers—one to dump over Josie's blond hair and another over Matt's thick skull.

"Thanks," she said stiffly as she took the cold mug. His hand lingered on hers an instant too long, and she saw how she could get even. She smiled up at Chad.

"You know," he said, grinning, "you really turn me on."

Any other time she'd have flashed him an indignant

look and turned away, but she was so furious. Matt said she should stay away from Chad. Well, what about him staying away from Josie?

She tried to make her smile even more inviting. Maybe it was unfair to use him to make Matt jealous, but Josie was still hanging on to Matt.

"I hope you don't mind my hugging Matty," Josie called out to Joanna. "We're old friends, aren't we, Matty?" She giggled and squeezed him.

Joanna darted a phony smile at them, noticing that Josie was smoking a joint—but then so were lots of the others.

Everyone was waiting to see what might happen.

"Yeah, old friends," Matt said, smiling, finally trying to untangle Josie's arm from him.

Why didn't he see Josie's game? He was supposed to be such a genius. Well, she'd like to shake him until his brains rattled.

She turned to Chad and took a long sip of beer.

"Easy," he said. "Take it easy."

"Sure." She drained the whole mug.

Chad took it to fill it again. "Matt's not the only guy in the world, you know."

She looked up at him. "I've been noticing." She had to get away before the situation got worse. "Want to go for a walk along the beach?"

His blue eyes widened in astonishment. "Why not?" He filled his mug so full the foam ran down over and clung to his hand.

She felt him following her through the crowd and hoped that Matt noticed.

As Chad closed the wooden gate behind them, she saw that Matt hadn't noticed their leaving at all. He was far too busy having fun with Josie. Well, plenty of the others had seen them. He'd find out sooner or later!

Orange and gold streaks of sunset moved down, splashing their brilliance across the dark ocean, still faintly lighting the beach. As she and Chad walked down to the water, she wondered how she could feel so empty, so awful in the midst of such beauty.

She felt Chad's arm slip around her waist and she quickly pulled it away, then reached apologetically to hold his hand.

"Am I moving too fast for you?" he asked.

She knew he wasn't talking about how quickly he was walking. "I don't know."

She stopped and sipped the cool beer. Maybe it was stupid to try to be good, to be Matt's girl. Maybe Josie's attitude was right: do whatever you feel like doing. Don't worry about anyone but yourself. She recalled discussing philosophy in her life education class.

"What's your philosophy of life, Chad?" she asked.

He laughed. "My philosophy of life? You're kidding!"

"No."

He looked at her quizzically, then shrugged. "All I'm really interested in is having a good time."

She felt his hand tightening on hers. "Would you like to kiss me now for fun?" she asked.

He stared at her against the brilliant sunset.

She looked down for a moment, kicking the sand, wondering what she was letting herself in for, then smiled up at him.

"Yeah," he said, hoarse. "I'd like to kiss you. I've been wanting to kiss you for a long time."

She felt trapped, but there seemed no way to stop now. She turned her face up to him.

He nearly lifted her from her feet, then his lips were hard against hers.

What was she doing? she thought frantically. She

didn't love him at all! She tried to push him away, but his shoulders were firm against her fists. As she finally pushed away, she saw someone had come out after them. He stopped and stood watching them.

"Matt!" Chad spat out.

She stared at Matt for a moment, then ran wildly to him. She'd explain how jealous he and Josie had made her. "Matt!" she shouted, but he was running for his house. "Matt! Wait . . ." Her feet sank into the dry sand on the hilly incline to his house, slowing her, and she thought she'd never catch up to him. "I have to talk to you, Matt," she yelled as he reached the patio gate.

He turned, furious. "There's no sense in talking. You're just like Melanie!"

Joanna stopped, shocked.

He opened the gate, glared at her as if he hated her, and was gone.

She walked slowly to the back of the fence and sank down on the sand. How could he compare her with Melanie? She and Chad had only been kissing. *Matt must have seen me push Chad away,* she thought, then remembered: he had probably seen her turn her face up for Chad's kiss, too.

Chad ambled over. "He must be mad."

She nodded. "Furious."

"I'd better talk to him." He looked out at the darkening sky, and for a long time there was only the roar of the ocean between them. "I'll tell him it was my fault."

"But it wasn't, Chad."

He laughed harshly. "I'll tell him women can't resist me."

Joanna tried to smile without much success. "Thanks. But I don't think it'll do any good."

He shrugged, and she watched him disappear around the fence.

Closing her eyes, she could still hear Matt's voice. *You're just like Melanie!* She remembered the day on the beach when he'd heard about Melanie's suicide. He'd been in such agony, which was exactly how she felt now.

She wished she could cry.

Couples slipped out from the enclosed patio to sit on the sand, bringing their mugs of beer. She scooted away, around the corner of the patio wall where no one would see her. If only Chad could convince Matt to come out to talk, maybe they could make up. She could already imagine herself melting into Matt's arms.

Moments later, her heart leaped as she heard his voice by the gate. He *was* coming out! He was coming to her! After getting up, she started around the fence.

Matt and Josie were hanging on to each other, Josie giggling softly as she looked up at him.

They didn't even see her, she thought, stepping back. They were carrying their beer mugs, heading out to the water's edge.

Stunned, she watched as they walked along the beach. The ocean's roar engulfed her, roaring louder and louder until it surrounded her like a black fury. He would be sorry! She would make Matt Thompson so sorry!

Chad plodded around the corner with two overflowing mugs of beer, his face grim. "No luck. He says he doesn't care."

Joanna whirled away, trembling with hurt and anger.

He waited for a while. "You want your beer?"

She nodded, reaching for it. She had to hold the cold glass mug with both hands, they shook so. She looked up at Chad.

He stood before her like a dejected sheep dog.

She was suddenly laughing, or maybe it was tearless crying. Finally she took a sip of beer with her lips quivering against the cold glass. Her throat stuck together and she could hardly swallow. At last she got it down. "It was fun while it lasted," she said.

Chad dropped down on the sand. "I wouldn't know."

She glanced at him. "Who's your date tonight anyhow?"

"I don't have one."

She drank deeply, then smiled at him in the last glimmering light. "You do now. If you want one."

He scooted over beside her in the sand. "You're crazy."

"Did you just figure that out?" She reached over to touch his square chin. It was smooth, but her fingers felt the tough dark beard that grew beneath the skin. "You've been shaving for a long time, haven't you?"

He caught her hand and held it to his chin. "Yeah."

They sat like that for a long moment, then she made her decision. "Well, let's drink up."

He was still staring at her when she emptied her mug. "Come here," he said.

She giggled. "Why don't you come and get me?"

As his arms closed around her, she put her hands over her mouth and giggled. "I do believe that first I'd like a little more beer."

Hours later she found herself groggy, staggering across the hard, wet sand at the water's edge with Chad. It was dark. Only a sliver of moon lit the starless sky.

"You're drunk!" he yelled above the ocean's roar. "I told you it was too much beer!"

She didn't quite understand. "Where's Matt? I want to see Matt." She reeled, waves of nausea welling up to her throat. "I'm going to throw up!" She vomited and sank down onto the sand, throwing up over and over. It was Matt's fault. He was the one who had started it all! He and that Josie!

She finally sat up.

Where was everyone? Where was Chad now?

She saw car headlights in Matt's driveway. They flooded the house, making it look like something from another planet. She got up shakily and staggered across the sand toward the lights.

She thought she saw Chad on the driveway, then she did hear his voice. He sounded drunk too. "Great party!" he was yelling.

Why was he leaving her? He'd kissed her. He'd kissed her a lot behind the fence. He said he'd been wild about her for a long time, that he had thought she was such a nice girl, and that maybe Matt would be lucky this time.

Suddenly she was crying.

Where was Matt? Oh, where was he?

She swayed and staggered around to the far side of the house so no one would see her. Matt had shown her where they hid the key. She had to find him!

Fumbling with the key, she dropped it twice before it slid into the keyhole. Then she was finally inside the house. Her mind reeled as she tottered through the white laundry room to the gleaming stainless steel kitchen, then to the den. Glancing in through the door, she could hardly believe the scene before her. She stood, swaying, holding on to the wall.

Matt was kissing Josie on the couch—on the brown leather couch where she and Matt had so often held each other . . . on *their* couch!

"Matt!" she cried out, her voice breaking.

He glanced up at her over Josie's blond hair. "Get

out!" he said. "You're *kishing* Chad . . . my friend Chad."

"I am not," she said, then remembered that she had. "It's your fault! Your fault, Matthew Thompson! You made me do it."

"Get out!" he shouted. "I'm *kishing* Josie."

Josie turned to her with a smug smile.

Well, she would not even talk to her. "Drunk! Matt Thompson's drunk!" Joanna screamed at him.

He laughed. "Eberybody's drunk. *Eberybody's* drunk."

"Take me home, Matt," she pleaded, tears bursting to her eyes again. "Take me home."

"Go home *yourshelf*, Melanie!" he yelled. "Go home, Melanie!"

Melanie! She wanted to tell him she was Joanna, not Melanie! That Melanie was dead and maybe it was his fault, too. That she was glad she hadn't given him Melanie's note from her wastebasket! But he was looking at her so hatefully she couldn't say a word.

Sobbing, she turned away and groped her way back to the kitchen. She had to get home. She would have to call someone, but not her parents.

David. She'd call David. He'd be glad to help her. He wasn't like Matt and Chad. She finally got the phone off the hook and dialed his number.

David answered sleepily.

"It's me, David," she sobbed. "Joanna." She concentrated on sounding sober. "You've got to get me . . . from Matt's house."

There was silence, then he sounded wide awake. "I'll be right there, Joanna. Just hold on."

Her head spun as she got the receiver back in place. There was a mug half full of beer on the kitchen counter. Maybe she'd feel better if she drank it. Drinking always made her feel better for a while, anyhow.

She gulped the beer quickly, then ran for the side door as the beer rushed back up her throat. Outside she vomited again.

She remembered crawling to the front curb, heaving dryly. David would find her, she thought, and the next thing she knew David was lifting her into his car.

He sat her down and patted her face. "Are you all right? Should I take you to the hospital?"

"No! No hospital!" Everybody would know.

He buckled her into the seat belt.

"I knew . . . I knew you'd come," she managed. "Have go home . . . Have go home . . ." Tears rolled down her cheeks. "I just drinking, David . . . just drinking beer." It was all she could remember until he was helping her out of his car at his house.

"Listen, Joanna, I can't take you to your house like this. I'll make you coffee downstairs." He nearly carried her to the side door, to the rec room where he'd had the church party.

"Waf—waf your friends see me?"

"There's no one here," he said, settling her on the couch. "Only my parents sleeping upstairs." He covered her with an afghan. "I'll go get you some coffee. I'll be back right away."

She shook her head at him, tears streaming down her face. "Matt doesh—doeshn't love me."

"God loves you, Joanna," David said, looking near tears himself. "God loves you."

"No, no . . ." *God couldn't love me,* she thought. The image of Chad kissing her on the beach came to her, then Matt standing there, watching them. She was awful. Matt didn't even love her now. How could God?

"God loves you," David insisted. "Now just stay here while I go for some coffee."

She watched him leave and glanced around, not sure where she was. Getting up, she staggered to the sliding glass door and looked outside.

The swimming pool shimmered in the starlit night.

She pushed the glass door open, little by little, until she could squeeze through. Slowly, slowly she tottered to the water. She was a drunk just like her father. Matt didn't love her anymore. He loved Josie now . . . he loved Josie.

The dark water gleamed like shiny black satin.

Maybe if she'd shown Matt that note from Melanie's wastebasket this wouldn't have happened. Maybe she was being punished. Could it be that Matt was right? That somehow she was turning into Melanie?

She looked down at the dark water and saw Melanie's face.

Don't be afraid, Melanie whispered to her. *Don't be afraid, Joanna.* Melanie was smiling. How beautiful she was. *Come with me. See how sorry Matt will be then.*

Slowly the darkness moved toward her, and she was falling like a star spiraling from the night sky. The silvery darkness reached up to her, engulfed her. Warm, so warm. Warmth surrounded her like a soft blanket, soothing away her agony in a velvety blackness.

At the last instant she saw Cathy's horrified face. Cathy would never in her life forget this . . . she might even follow!

I want to live! her mind screamed, but it was too late.

————

When she came to, she was lying on the wet concrete, water rushing from her mouth as someone pressed on her back.

It was dark, but not as dark as in the water. Starlight. A starlit night. She shivered.

David . . . he was trying to save her. He was sobbing over her.

"David?"

"How could you, Joanna?" he asked.

"She was calling me," she whispered. "Melanie said I'd make Matt so sorry."

"Heavenly Father," David prayed, "we take authority over the power of Satan *now,* in the name of Jesus!"

"Was it the devil?" she asked. She was certain she'd heard Melanie calling from the dark water, and she'd seen her. "Melanie was so beautiful, and she wanted me to be with her."

David was praying, praying, praying as he lifted her. He carried her slowly across the yard to the rec room and finally put her down on the couch.

"It's too late for praying," she tried to tell him as she lay down on the couch. God could never forgive her for whatever had just happened.

"It's never too late," David said. "God loves you. He can forgive anything. You only have to speak to Him through Jesus."

"Through Jesus?"

"You have to accept Jesus . . . just accept Jesus."

"I want to, David," she whispered. "Somehow I've always wanted to, but I never—I never really understood."

"Just ask Him to come into your heart, to forgive you and blot out the past. He'll do it, Joanna, but you have to ask Him." Tears were running down his face. "Do you want to get on your knees?"

She sat up on the couch weakly, but she wanted to get down on her knees. As she slowly knelt, water ran from her wet clothes, making a puddle all around her.

"I accept Jesus," she whispered, crying. "I accept Jesus."

"Ask Him to come into your heart," David sobbed, kneeling beside her.

"Please come into my heart, Jesus," she begged. "Please come into my heart. Forgive me . . . forgive me . . . my sins."

After a while she looked at David and knew he was praying for her. His shirt and jeans were dripping wet, and tears streamed down his cheeks, but his face glowed with hope.

She thought that something miraculous should be happening, that God would do something, but she still felt wet and cold and aching and wretched. David looked over at her as if he expected something to happen, too.

She did feel better, and David had insisted that God would forgive her. "I guess I'd better go home," she finally said. "Yes, I better go home now."

15

$\mathcal{A}$t two o'clock the next afternoon, Joanna could scarcely pull herself from bed when Matt called. She was certain that she'd never felt so awful in all of her life. Slowly she began to recall David sneaking her home last night. Luckily no one had seen her.

Her mother looked worried as Joanna plodded out to the hall phone. "You must have the flu," she said. "You look so pale."

"I'll be all right, Mom, don't worry." But the truth was she felt like a zombie. She wasn't even sure she wanted to talk to Matt. In her mind's eye she could still see him with Josie on the den couch. But he had seen her kissing Chad, too. If only she could forget the whole miserable night. If only there was a way to erase it all.

Picking up the phone, she managed a cool "Hello."

"I didn't know if you'd be talking to me," Matt said. She didn't answer.

"I should have cut off Josie right away," he said, "but I started drinking when they brought the keg. You know, when you went shopping. I'm sorry. I want to see you."

Just hearing Josie's name infuriated Joanna. She could still see her walking onto the patio and hugging Matt.

There was a long silence, and Joanna was determined not to be the one to break it. She could imagine Matt now, probably in that stainless steel kitchen, alone as usual, which began to melt her resolve. He was always alone

157

now. "When did you want to see me?" she finally asked.

"Now?" he asked.

She felt too awful. She just wanted to go back to bed and forget everything. "No, not now."

"Can I take you to dinner at Morelli's? Please, Joanna."

She wondered what had happened to Josie, but this was no time to ask. "Okay, Matt. But not until six o'clock."

As she hung up, she wondered if he didn't have a hangover, too. Of course, he hadn't tried to drown himself on top of drinking.

The phone rang again as soon as she hung up. "Are you all right, Joanna?" David asked.

"I've been better," she admitted, embarrassed. "Thanks for everything, David."

"I want to see you," he said, "but we're going to visit friends of the family. I can't get out of it."

"I'll be okay," she told him, though she wasn't too sure.

At least the house was quiet, wonderfully quiet. She could go back to bed, she thought. Cathy was at Dede's house and wouldn't be asking questions.

———

Matt looked angry when he picked her up, and she couldn't imagine why. He'd been the one pleading with her to go out. When they were in the car, she realized he'd been drinking again, maybe all day long.

"Let's kiss and make up," he said, his words slurring.

Joanna cringed. His breath smelled foul; his cheeks were flushed. She edged away to her door. "I'm sorry about what happened, too, Matt," she said. "It was stupid. We were both stupid."

"You don't look very sorry sitting on that side of the car," he told her.

"It's just that my stomach is queasy, and you smell like a brewery."

"*You're* criticizing?" His green eyes flattened with anger, and he squared his jaw as he started the car. He pulled out onto the road so fast that the tires squealed. "*You* were pretty drunk last night yourself!"

"I'd like to forget the whole thing," she said. "I'm really sorry."

"It's hard for me to forget you and Chad," Matt said. "You're supposed to be my girl. Chad's supposed to be my friend!"

She decided not to answer. It wasn't going to be easy for either of them to forget. Maybe they would never get over last night.

Matt looked furious as he drove. "Can you imagine how I felt, seeing you two kissing on the beach?"

"It hurt me to see you with Josie, too."

He didn't seem to hear. "It almost killed me to see you with Chad!"

"It almost killed me to see you with Josie, too! She started the whole thing!"

Why couldn't they just make up? Joanna thought. She looked at Matt. He was so hurt and angry. "Do you think we'll ever forgive each other?"

"I don't know," he said dully. He swung the car onto a road overlooking a steep canyon.

"Where are we?" she asked, looking farther down the road. Cars were parked under eucalyptus trees, and couples in the cars were wrapped in each other's arms.

"It's the water district road," he said.

She had a feeling Matt had been here before. "Is this where you bring girls like Josie?" she snapped. She was sorry as soon as the words were out of her mouth.

Darting a furious look at her, he parked the car alongside the road, then moved toward her.

She backed away.

"I only want something in the glove compartment," he said angrily. He reached into it and pulled out a flask. "I need a drink. How about you?"

Joanna's stomach turned over. "What is it?"

"Bourbon."

She shook her head. She didn't want a drink at all.

She watched him tilt the flask to his mouth, his Adam's apple bobbing as he swallowed. Today it looked disgusting. Just the smell of the liquor made her stomach churn.

"Look, Matt, I don't want to sit here," she said. "I thought we were going to Morelli's."

He turned to her, his green eyes hard, then gulped from the flask again.

What had happened to the happy Matt he used to be? Had it all been an act? Sure, lots had gone wrong in his life, and she hadn't helped matters last night.

She took a deep breath. Okay, she'd try again to make up. "Please forgive me about last night, Matt. I really forgive you." Saying the words, she felt that somehow they were beginning to come true.

"What's wrong?" he asked nastily. "You want a drink after all?" He pushed the flask at her.

"That's not it at all," she protested.

Ignoring her, he screwed the lid back on and threw the flask into the glove compartment.

"Matt, I'm trying to apologize!"

He backed the car out wildly. As he floored the gas pedal, they went weaving onto the road.

"Stop this, Matt!" she shouted.

At the end of the road there was only a barbed-wire fence in front of a deep canyon. The car roared to it.

"Matt!" Joanna screamed.

Grinning, he squealed the car to a stop.

"Think I'd drive over the cliff?" he asked with a laugh as he looked out over the rocky canyon.

"Please don't be like this," she pleaded.

He was intent on the canyon below. "Maybe you don't know the real me."

She reached out and touched his hand. "I really like the real you."

"Yeah?" Taking her hand, he squeezed it hard.

"You're hurting me!" She couldn't believe he could be like this. It was as if he were two different people. She wondered how many pain pills he had taken today.

"Let's go to Morelli's," he said.

For an instant she felt a wave of relief, then he drove away crazily. She sat with her hands clenched all the way to the restaurant.

Inside, they were seated in a window booth, and Matt told the waitress, "We'll have a bottle of red wine."

"I don't want any," Joanna said quietly. "I guess I'll have a glass of milk."

Matt frowned at her.

"I'm afraid I'll have to ask for your ID," the waitress told Matt.

Joanna watched in amazement as he dug for his wallet and pulled out his driver's license. He handed it to the waitress nonchalantly. What was he doing? He was seventeen. She knew that for certain.

The waitress looked at his license, then at Matt several times.

After she left, Joanna whispered, "How did you pull that off?"

He grinned. "I'm twenty-one."

This is ridiculous, she thought. She'd seen his license. He was definitely seventeen.

"Okay, you're twenty-one," she agreed, to be done with the subject.

But Matt didn't want to drop the discussion. "It's a Tijuana Special," he said. "Your friend Chad and I went over the border for them last summer. In fact, it says I'm almost twenty-two."

How much more didn't she know about him? He'd never mentioned the phony license.

The waitress darted a suspicious glance at him when she brought the bottle of wine. It was far too quiet as she placed a wineglass in front of him and poured the red wine.

After she had left, Joanna whispered, "You didn't fool her."

Matt didn't answer, but his eyes raked her harshly. He downed the first glass of wine and quickly poured another, then dug out his pills.

Joanna stared at him. "Matt, you shouldn't."

He popped two of the pills into his mouth and swallowed them with the wine. "I've been doing it for months. Hasn't hurt me yet."

She didn't believe him. It was her fault he was doing this. She'd hurt him so badly last night.

After the waitress brought their pizza, Joanna tried to concentrate on eating, but she could hardly swallow.

Matt ate one slice of pizza, then sat drinking wine.

They seemed to be sitting there forever, she thought. She glanced around at the people in Morelli's, hoping that someone might stop by to pull Matt out of this mood, but it was still early. There were mostly families at the tables.

"Maybe we'd better go," she suggested.

"Not done yet," he said. The wine bottle was still a third full.

She sat back. "Sorry."

He didn't answer.

She would have to drive, she decided. She didn't have her driver's license with her, but that was too bad.

As he tried to pour another glass of wine, he bumped the goblet, nearly tipping it over. He set the bottle down hard. His words slurred. "How'd you go home?"

He meant last night, she thought, not wanting to tell him about calling David. She started to get up. "Let's go home, Matt. I'm tired."

He stood up and, reaching over the table, pushed her down in her seat. "How'd you go home last night?"

"Let's talk about it in the car," she said, "not here."

"Talking now!" he yelled.

"Please, Matt. Everyone is looking at us!"

He shouted, "Who took you home?"

She saw the waitress getting Mr. Morelli from the kitchen.

Joanna stood up. "Come on. Let's go home."

Mr. Morelli looked grim as he hurried toward them, his voluminous white apron still tied around his waist. "Everything all right here?" he asked.

"No!" Matt shouted. "She's my girl!"

Joanna tugged at Matt, certain that everyone in the restaurant had noticed. Someone in a booth at the far wall was standing up to see what was going on.

"Very beautiful girl, too," Mr. Morelli said, helping Matt up. "I'd like you to have dinner on the house, you're such a handsome couple." He was expertly ushering Matt out by the elbow, smiling and talking pleasantly while Joanna trailed behind them.

She could see people staring at them, disgust on their faces. As they approached the door, people waiting for tables gaped, and she thought they would never get out.

Finally they were outside, and Morelli's Christmas

lights blinked at them in the darkness. "Thank you," she said to Mr. Morelli.

Matt looked confused, then saw where he was. "Hey—"

"Don't bother to come back," Mr. Morelli interrupted. "I could lose my license, lose the whole restaurant over a kid like you." He rushed back in, slamming the door behind him.

Joanna grabbed Matt's arm, trying to hurry him through the dark parking lot. "I'll drive," she said as they stopped on the driver's side of his car.

He stood digging in his pocket for the car keys. "I'm driving," he answered, but he could hardly stand.

"You never let me drive," she protested.

He slapped her face. "David picked you up!"

She held her burning cheek, backing away from him. "How did you know?"

"I guessed," he said, shoving her roughly into the car, past the steering wheel, and to the passenger side. "How dumb do you think I am?" His eyes were wild in the light of the open car door. He slammed it and started the motor. The radio blared.

There was no time to fasten her seat belt before they lurched forward, then careened crazily through the parking lot.

"Please, Matt!"

He pealed out onto the road and floored the gas pedal.

"Where are we going?" she shouted over the rock music.

"You go with nobody but me!" he yelled.

He sounded crazy, she thought, looking out in terror. The road was completely dark. "Your lights! Turn on the headlights!"

He turned them on and glared at her as if it were her fault.

She tried to concentrate on the road ahead, glad there was little traffic. On the radio a singer wailed about how rotten love was—and Joanna agreed with him.

Matt suddenly slowed down and whipped the car around a corner.

"Where are we going?" Suddenly she recognized the road and the eucalyptus trees whizzing by in the glare of their headlights. It was the dead-end water district road leading out over the canyon.

The car was going faster and faster, flat out now.

"Matt!" she screamed. "Stop!"

He looked crazy, as if he weren't hearing her at all.

"No, Matt, no!" She grabbed his leg, pulling his foot from the gas pedal.

Their headlights pierced the darkness, shining on the barbed-wire fence at the end of the road.

Joanna tugged desperately at the steering wheel, pulling it toward her as hard as she could, her mind screaming, *God help me! God help me!*

At the last moment she felt the car turning away from the canyon, turning, then suddenly flipping. . . . She was against the door, flying out, somersaulting into the night, the car crashing through the darkness beyond her.

For a long time there was only gray shadowy silence.

When she finally opened her eyes, she saw fire from the smashed car flaring up a eucalyptus tree, lighting everything around them. They hadn't gone over the cliff into the canyon!

She pulled herself from a brambly bush and stumbled toward the flickering firelight. "Matt!" she screamed.

She nearly tripped over his body. "Matt, oh, Matt."

She collapsed on her knees beside him. "Please, God, let him be okay! Please, God!"

He was so still, sprawled out on his back in the weeds by the roadside. What could she do?

The crackling fire spread rapidly along the row of eucalyptus trees, each one bursting into flames like a giant torch. She felt frantic. She had to do something. Quite suddenly, she remembered David's prayer. "Please let him be alive, God. In Jesus' name, please let him be alive!"

She kissed Matt's forehead and saw his lashes flutter. He might be hurt badly, but he was alive!

In the distance fire engines screamed through the night. Someone had seen the fire. Firemen would know what to do for Matt.

"It's okay," she said. "Everything's going to be all right!"

He tried to smile.

"We're alive, Matt! We're alive!"

She'd never been so thankful in all her life. "Oh, God, thank you," she cried out, tears of gratitude welling in her eyes. "Thank you, God, thank you!" she called out, and a wondrous joy leaped through her. She was surrounded by love as she had never felt it before. And she knew, without even thinking, that this was God's embrace, that God had touched her with His love. With a strange clarity she understood she would never be the same again, not now or through eternity.

Matt was still conscious, lying on the hard ground, when the fire engine and then, later, the ambulance arrived. As the white-suited attendants lifted him onto a stretcher, Joanna said, "He's going to be all right."

The attendants eyed her strangely as they laid her on the stretcher.

She was smiling as the grayness moved toward her, still smiling as everything became black.

16

For a long time there was only darkness and confusion. Then Joanna saw the surge of light and heard the glorious singing. "Morning is broken, like the first morning. Blackbird has spoken, like the first bird. . . ." Bells rang out joyously across the earth and heavens, echoing and re-echoing from planet to planet, sunset to sunset, mountain peak to mountain peak. Her heart joined the clouds of choirs coming down in great light with Jesus. "Joyful, joyful, we adore Thee, God of glory, Lord of love. . . ."

Jesus was coming to her, strong as a carpenter, His eyes welling with tenderness. His arms moved out to her in welcome, and she knew, without hearing a word, that she was to follow Him.

Standing in the multitude behind Jesus, her grandfather was smiling at her, and she remembered a song he had taught her when she was little. She sang out loudly now, with all her heart, in offering to Him, "Oh, how I love Jesus. Oh, how I love Jesus . . ."

She was moving to Him now in the power of love, floating across earth. *Let me go with you now,* she thought. *Let me go with you now!*

"Joanna! Joanna!" someone was calling.

Slowly, slowly Jesus moved away, receding with the multitudes as easily as billowing fog moves over the sea.

She seemed to be going backward through a tunnel,

away from the great light. When He was gone there was only darkness.

"Joanna? Joanna?" her mother called out, her voice quavering.

She opened her eyes and saw her parents and David hovering over her hospital bed.

David was beaming, but her mother's and father's eyes were red, full of tears.

A nurse leaned over to take Joanna's pulse. "It's not often that our patients wake up singing."

"What was I singing?" she asked.

"Something about Jesus," the nurse answered.

"You were singing 'Oh, How I Love Jesus,'" David put in. He turned to the nurse. "Do things like that happen often in hospitals?"

The nurse shook her head slightly, as if she were still stunned. "Sometimes. You know, when people are on the edge, surprising things can happen. I'll notify the doctors. And I'll tell Cathy out in the waiting room, too."

"What did the nurse mean, 'on the edge'?" Joanna asked.

Her mother blinked hard, turning to Joanna's father.

Her father cleared his throat, but his words trembled. "The doctors didn't think you'd live, Joanna. Not one of them thought you had a chance for the last two days."

He glanced at David. "David prayed and prayed for you, and Cathy's probably still praying now. Even your mother and I prayed."

Joanna remembered. "I saw Grandfather for a moment, just a moment. He looked so happy and so beautiful. That's why I sang 'Oh, how I love Jesus.' Grandfather taught me that a long time ago."

Her father nodded. "He taught me that a long time ago, too."

"Did you see Him?" David asked, and she knew that he meant Jesus.

She closed her eyes and could see Him again in her memory. "He was so beautiful, so tenderhearted, so full of love. But I don't know why He chose me. I just don't understand."

"Jesus explained it in the Bible," David said. " 'The wind blows wherever it pleases. You hear its sound, but cannot tell where it comes from and where it is going. So it is with everyone born of the Spirit.' "

Yes, she thought. God's spirit had come to touch her heart like a great wind that appeared from nowhere. No one knew where a wind came from or where it might go next. She tried to recall exactly how it had happened.

First, she'd accepted Jesus at David's house. And she'd knelt in thanksgiving at Matt's side by the road, thanking God that Matt was still alive, thanking Him joyously. And then, like a great wind, God's love had come upon her.

"Can it happen to everyone?" she asked David.

He nodded. "If they open their hearts and accept Jesus. Gramps said it isn't always such a dramatic conversion. Usually it comes slowly, being attracted more and more to Jesus."

Her father's voice was reflective. "Joanna's grandfather said it came slowly to him, that he was drawn to Jesus until being a Christian was the most important thing in his life."

Then that's what has been happening to Cathy, Joanna thought.

"It's a great wonder, no matter how it comes," David said. "At least that's what Gramps always claimed."

"David says it's what people call being born again," her father explained.

"Except that most people don't really know what *born again* means," David said. "I think it's one of those things like love or sadness or pain. You don't know what it is until you have it yourself."

"It's a wonderful glow of . . ." Joanna struggled to find the right word.

"Love?" David suggested.

"Yes," she said, "it's a wonderful glow of God's love that blots away everything bad you've ever done and fills you to overflowing."

"That's what my . . . my sister said years ago," her mother said. "But when Annie quit taking her heart medicine and put herself in God's hands—and died"— she was suddenly crying—"I fought and fought religion. I fought God when it was *Annie* who stopped taking the medicine."

"Gramps said everyone fights God," David replied. "We want to be in charge."

"I see now how crazy that is," Joanna said. "I've never felt so happy in my life."

She was smiling when she slowly drifted off to sleep.

Hours later, when she awakened, they were still there, and she realized that her hatred for her father was gone. He caught her hand and held it. "When the doctors said you probably wouldn't live, that it would take a miracle, I promised—" He couldn't go on and held his handkerchief to his trembling lips for a long time. "I promised God that if you lived, that if you would be all right again, I would never touch alcohol again. I know I can keep that promise with His help."

She squeezed his hand, her eyes bright with tears, and reached for her mother's hand. Joanna shyly put their hands together, and they were suddenly in each other's arms.

David smiled at her, embarrassed. "Heidi called. She sends her love."

Joanna dimly remembered the afternoon she and Cathy had gone riding with Heidi. Heidi must have sensed that something was terribly wrong with them that day, and she'd tried to help them forget. *Someday,* Joanna thought, *Heidi is going to need help. Someday she is going to have to face people instead of horses.* Strange as it seemed, Joanna felt ready to be her friend.

"How is Matt?" she asked. Her parents and David glanced at each other as if they didn't know whether they should tell. She'd been so certain he would be all right, so certain. She made herself ask, "Is he dead?"

"No," her father answered. "He's still alive. But the doctors aren't sure that he'll live. If he does, they say he'll never walk again. He'll always be in a wheelchair."

"It's his spine," her mother explained. "He's paralyzed from the neck down."

Strange, Joanna thought. She had been so convinced that he'd be all right.

————

It wasn't until two days later that Joanna's doctor allowed her to walk down the hospital corridor to the intensive care ward. She wore the new yellow robe that Cathy had chosen for her, as bright yellow as her joy.

"Only five minutes," the nurse warned Joanna as she led her around to Matt's curtained cubicle. "He's hanging in a Stryker frame."

Seeing him, she gasped. He hung facedown, toward the white tile hospital floor, in a hideous slinglike contraption.

"Matt," she whispered, bending to him.

His green eyes opened with recognition, then closed quickly.

Please, God, she prayed, *let me say the right words to Matt. He looks so miserable.* She got down on the cold floor, lying nearly under him so she could look up into his face.

His eyes were still closed, but his lips trembled.

"God loves you, Matt," she said. "He loves you."

Matt's voice was hard. "I'm being punished. I'm being punished for Melanie . . . for trying to kill you and myself . . . for all the rotten things I've done in my life."

She shook her head, looking up at him. "You're punishing yourself. David says God can forgive anything . . . anything!"

He had to understand God loved him. He could die any minute. "God will forgive you, Matt."

He looked as if he might cry. "Do you forgive me, Joanna?"

"Of course, I forgive you. I forgive you with all my heart!"

Matt opened his eyes with hope.

She wanted to cry for the pain he'd endured the past few years. He thought no one loved him . . . not his mother and sisters, who'd moved away . . . not his father, who was too busy . . . not Melanie, who had killed herself . . . and then not even Joanna Stevens.

"Do you really forgive me?" he asked with a catch in his voice.

Her eyes were wet with tears. "I forgive you."

He managed a thin smile.

"I'm guilty, too, about Melanie," Joanna said. "That night at her party I found a strange note in her wastebasket. I even wondered if it might be a suicide note. So I was guilty, too. I should have told you about her note—you might have saved her. But I didn't tell you, and it tormented me. I think that's part of why I started drinking too much. I was trying to hide my guilt." She looked up at him again. "Maybe that's why you started taking so many pills and drinking so much. You felt full of guilt, too."

"Maybe," he whispered.

"David says Melanie was responsible to God for her own actions. We weren't entirely responsible for her." It was so important that he had this right. "Do you understand, Matt? Each person has to get right with God."

"Yeah," he said, his voice full of anguish. "But I tried to kill us!" He looked as if he could see it all again.

"God will forgive anything if we're truly sorry." She was surprised at understanding so fast. "He loves you, Matt."

There was a long silence. Then his lower lip quivered. "Thanks . . . for turning the . . . steering wheel."

Her eyes filled with tears of joy. "Oh, Matt, I'm so glad you're thanking me! It means you're glad we're alive!"

He looked at her closely. "Something's happened to you. You look different . . . more beautiful. It's your eyes."

She beamed. He could see it! He could see her joy! Even here on the cold hospital floor!

"The doctors call my being all right a miracle," she said. "It can happen to you, too."

His eyes brimming with tears, he said, "It's going to take a miracle."

"Yes," she answered softly. "It's going to take a miracle."

He smiled ruefully at her. "You know," he said after a while, "your eyes look like Rena's now."

Joanna's heart leapt at the sheer joy of the idea.

Rena, oh, Rena! she thought, remembering the first time she'd seen her. Rena had been reading by the big ocean-front window. She must have been praying too because her eyes had been luminous, so golden with love.

Joanna saw the nurse coming. "One more minute, please?"

The nurse nodded.

"I have to go, Matt, but there's time to pray. Will you pray with me? Please, will you pray?"

He looked hopeful, despite tears that dropped straight down and splattered on the white tile floor. "Yeah, Joanna," he said with a wonder-struck catch in his voice. "Please, let's pray."

At a librarians' banquet, the words "whither the wind bloweth" came to Elaine so strongly that she knew it was meant to be the title of her next novel. No one in the room had spoken the words; the librarians at her table had never heard them. They looked at her strangely when she told them that perhaps her next novel had begun. Unfortunately she couldn't start a novel then. A year later as she stepped into a chapel in Mt. Hermon, California, an elderly black man was speaking from his pew. As she sat down in the pew behind him, she heard the end of his testimony: "whither the wind bloweth." She knew then it was time to begin. While she wrote WHITHER THE WIND BLOW-ETH, now entitled JOANNA, the words poured out of her as never before. It was as mysterious to her as how the title was given, as mysterious as from whither the winds blow.